Journey Train

Journey Train

Alecia D Agard

By-line

To order additional copies of this book, contact:
Xlibris Corporation
0-800-644-6988
www.XlibrisPublishing.co.uk
Orders@XlibrisPublishing.co.uk
303271

I would like to dedicate this book to the
memory of Tashan Wholas Spencer

Always in our hearts Tashan xx

I would like to thank Roy and Peter-Lee for their
help in the construction of this book.

Good luck to my beautiful nieces
Sade and Shanice Agard in their upcomming exams

Thanks to my son and family who always bring
sunshine, joy and happiness God bless

CHAPTER 1

Churchyard

The fierce wind cleared the autumn leaves revealing the old brick paving leading to the church, where the congregation sat huddled under black winter clothing listening to the chimes that silenced the priest as he walked over to sit in the chancel.

He then signalled by nodding to Scott the young boy sitting in the congregation with his mother, Linda; he immediately left his seat to stand at the altar. Looking across to the parishioners as he ruffled his pockets producing a crumpled piece of paper, which he unravelled slowly before clearing his throat:

"You were my friend. I will miss you dearly. I wished that you could stay, but you had to go away. I do not know what I will do. I'm really going to miss you." Bowing his head, he walked back down the aisle noticing the tears of the congregation from his poem.

Linda and Scott strolled out the cemetery towards their modest black car after the funeral.

"I can't believe he's gone now." Scott wept to his distraught mother.

"He's not gone Scott! He's just fallen asleep." She said whilst dabbing her eyes with a used tissue.

"I wonder what heavens really like . . . How do we get there?" Scott asked.

Linda was unsure about the answer, but knew the beliefs were more positive.

"There are many mysteries in this world that we may struggle to find an answer for that's because we are physical, but there's a spiritual side to us and spiritually we will find the answers in our beliefs." She said.

CHAPTER 2

Leaving Earth

Linda and Scott were determined not to forget Mowgli and they returned to his grave a week later to lay flowers. Driving back from the cemetery there was a loud scream as a bright light appeared that transferred them above the clouds and the dark universe with them remaining completely unaware.

Dense clouds of fog in the mist projected over the horizon whilst a cool fresh breeze blew away the deep, green leaves then slowly the fog cleared revealing a sandy, stony road set in grass that was deep jade in colour, surrounded by tall trees. Unique flowers with long, green stems attached to colourful petals were visible amongst the grass.

The beaming sun fused with a metal object which lay on the stony road resulting in a light shining brightly. Beneath the beam laid a battered, broken, black car with a cracked windscreen.

Inside, Linda's ruffled, black hair hid her bruised face where blood trickled; her first movement was her head, which displayed smudged, red lipstick and dark, black mascara which stained her face on turning over she revealed bloodstains penetrating her blouse.

Slowly her eyes rolled and then opened to reveal stunning blue eyes as blue as the deepest oceans.

She slowly wiped away the blood running down her face before the shock then horror overcame her, she sprang forward on her seat on noticing her young son strapped lifeless in the seat beside her covered in cuts and bruises.

"Scott, Scott." Linda shouted shaking him vigorously and then she screamed at him.

"Wake up!" When there was no response from him, she pushed at the car door it failed to open; she kicked it open then raced to the other side pulling him from the wreck; she dragged him to the grass shaking him again and then his eyes slowly opened. "Mum." He muttered.

Linda was enthralled to hear him say her name. "You will be ok!" She said whilst rummaging her bag until she had a tissue, which she used to clean his wounds. Remaining bewildered at the unfamiliarity that surrounded her as she pondered to recollect how she arrived at this deserted, mysterious place.

CHAPTER 3

The Accident

Linda's two children were her whole life; she struggled hard to keep them out of poverty.

The Manley Park was an over populated town that housed hundreds of the poorest people from different nationalities. It also had one of the highest crime rates in the country.

Scott was the youngest of her children, who was witty and charming with pale, white skin with large, brown freckles shading a large proportion of his face. He had a distinctive fiery, ginger, Mohican hair cut; he was fortunate to inherit his mother's deep, blue eyes and her winning smile that often won people over.

Scott a loving, likable, warm eleven-year-old boy with many talents his biggest was football. He was a strong player that was good in the air and gifted with pace which made him a cut above his fellow teammates.

Melting snow fixed on the ground fell weeks ago as Linda and Scott travelled to the under eleven league match where Scott would perform.

Many cars and trucks strolled past the small, black car whilst it journeyed along the motorway.

The heavily, loaded lorry speeded whilst loud music echoed from the cabin at the same time the reckless driver stuffed his face with crisps and drink then panicked when a metal object flew across the windscreen, prior to him realizing he had knife edged in to something.

His worst thoughts confirmed when he looked through the side window and saw the fragmented remains of a car.

It was Linda's car he had seen which made him pull over to dial for assistance. The emergency services sirens bellowed from their cars, trucks and vans as they forced their way through the heavy pile-ups. Their vehicles with flashing, blue lights blocked adjacent lanes with some stationed at the scene of the crash.

In the mist of the mayhem the paramedics and ambulance crew pumped away at Linda and Scott's chest. Whilst police photographed skid marks and scavenged for clues hoping to secure evidence of this dreadful accident.

Emily the eldest of Linda's children was a beautiful, young woman with stunning, long, black hair which accompanied her blue eyes inherited from her mother.

"My rock;" was how her mother described her, because she looked after her younger brother and maintained the house whilst her mother worked very long hours.

A lonely and worried Emily opened the street door of the family home. She was expecting her mother and her little brother, but to her dismay a police officer dressed in uniform adjusting her radio fixed tightly to her jacket confronted her.

"Are you, Emily Harris?" She asked. Emily remained silent startled by her presence; there was a bad feeling that came over her—something terrible had happened.

"Officer Smith! Can I come in?" She asked.

Emily nodded in response to the officer's question ahead of leading her to the living room where she fixed her eyes on family photographs exposing happy family days; she then focused on the plants dispatched in each corner ahead of noticing the dining table with the unusual, shaped, teardrop lamp as she sat on the black leather sofa.

"Come and sit down, Emily!" Officer Smith said then patted the seat beside her.

Emily accepted, but felt uncomfortable when noticing a compelling look on the officer's face.

"It's not good news!" Her head bowed before continuing. "Your mother and your brother were involved in an accident on the motorway." She announced her point of vision transfixed on Emily who was shattered on hearing the news, which made her pace up and down the living room rubbing her hands continuously until finally finding a seat at the table; where she set her eyes on the dim beam that seem to comfort her before turning to Officer Smith.

"My mother and my brother will they be ok?" She asked.

The police officer could only shrug her shoulders at that point; she struggled to find the correct words.

"There is still hope my dear . . . They are still with us." She replied.

CHAPTER 4

Nowhere

Meanwhile, Linda remained mystified by her surroundings whilst cleaning her face then combing her hair, with Scott across her lap.

The large trees, huge plants and the beautiful, unique flowers with stalks six feet tall engulfed her, before noticing an array of petals with bright colours suddenly transforming into huge butterflies and ladybirds.

She stopped combing her hair to fix her eyes on the beautiful creatures flying up to the skies; suddenly an abrupt change more extravagant petals transformed to butterflies and ladybirds then there was stillness for a while then another distraction, squawking noises further afield that caused Scott to fidget as the noise amplified.

"Did you hear that?" Linda whispered, but he was sleepy and dazed she got little response from him.

Her attention taken by a huge bird gliding through the clouds which she glimpsed before it vanished leaving her completely unaware that further afield the huge purple and golden-feathered creatures which resembled enormous lizards with wings began to land.

These gigantic birds had small, green heads, long beaks and three fingers attached to their wing claws.

Unexpectedly a different type of flying reptiles were appearing in the fields that looked like bats with teeth small and lacking and a long bony tail. Position on their hand was a distinguished fourth finger attached to a membrane that allowed them to fly rapidly.

Screeching, squawking and flapping were the prominent sounds as both types of reptiles filled the fields at the same time preparing for conflict.

The inpatient creatures attempted to fly off, only to return squawking uncontrollably then spreading their wings before fiercely attacking the different species amongst them with their teeth. They gashed into necks screeching and squawking loudly; the blood poured from the purple-feathered birds whose wings flapped uncontrollably before many lay lifeless in the fields.

The aftermath was horrific the blood continued to gush from the necks of the creatures and they continued to fall until only the bat type birds remained in the fields, which began eating the remains of their opponents.

The victorious birds flapped and squawked then flew up above the low clouds into the deep, blue sky leaving the fields empty once more. `

Scott lifted his head from his mother's lap on hearing a buzzing noise in his head; after rubbing his eyes he was terrified of what was coming towards them.

"Mum" Scott shouted pointing at the swarm of pigeon size bees.

"Get in the car Scott!" Linda panicked as they rushed for the broken down car with the bees continuing to follow.

"Wind the window up!" Scott shouted frantically on entering the car, but Linda struggled to close the window.

"It's jammed!" She shouted then forcefully tried to shut it, within minutes the huge bee entered buzzing crazily resulting in Linda and Scott screaming and shouting at the bee as it continued tormenting them.

". . . My bag!" Linda shouted pushing Scott away to grab her bag which she threw at the window that resulted in spores of fungi and bacteria spurting out of the bee. She pushed the remains through the gap and then tried the winder again this time the window closed. Relieved at what she encountered, she sighed ahead of rubbing her hands to clean the resilient fluid from the bee that had stained them.

Scott surprised by his mother's bravery that of which had made him extremely proud, continued peering at the bees outside.

"Where are we, mum?" He asked.

"I don't know, darling." She replied as she turned towards him.

Scott, still focused on bees buzzing now through the large trees was alerted to a building in the distance.

"There's a building over there, mum!' He shouted eagerly to his mother who stopped cleaning her hands and then looked through the tall trees across the acres of green fields at the construction.

"We need to find out what that structure is!" Linda replied focusing directly at the building.

Scott and Linda walked vigilantly through the tall, green grass after the entire bees had gone.

Subsequently a crack of lightening stuck which opened the entire skies; the clouds turned black then evaporated leaving them perplexed by what they had witnessed a large ball shaped cloud fell from the sky to form into a tall wizard with a huge, purple cloak and a tall, black, pointed hat.

On noticing Linda he removed his hat and bowed stylishly then lifted his head to reveal a serious, angry face which made her fearful.

"Ang-red, ang-red." He mumbled opening his cloak like a gigantic, purple bat then retrieving a crystal wand that he pointed at the open space; he raised his hands above his head and the grass blazed wildly.

Linda, afraid of the fire grabbed Scott and stood away from the intense heat that was choking them; she glanced at the wizard hoping he would put out the fire, looking back at her the fire continued to blaze.

Unexpectedly before their very eyes, smoke began to appear from the lake as it changed to every colour of the rainbow, almost resembling a huge chameleon before returning to its original state. The lake was calm for a short time and then miraculously the lake transformed into ice. The wizard threw his arms into the air, lifted his head to the skies, then stamped his feet in anger whilst Linda and Scott remained silent, fearful and bewildered.

*

"Alcatraz, Alcatraz." He mumbled.

The ice cracked and revealed a mirror the size of the lake inside appeared a young woman; she had beautiful flowing, dark hair with skin like snow; she danced and romped with a tall, dark, handsome, young man.

The angry wizard kicked the flowers and then thumbed the tree trunk ahead of flashing his wand at the mirror.

"Be gone!" He shouted.

Scott and Linda became stunned when a baby crocodile appeared and waddle onto the mirror which reverted to a huge waterfall, where a gigantic dinosaur emerged roaring before vanishing. Linda held Scott tightly when there was a loud bang and the waterfall let off an array of vibrant colours and then reverted to the mirror, where the trapped women appeared.

The wizard fixed his eyes on the dancing women and then turned to Linda she remained mystified.

"That's my adulterous wife who's been having an affair." He said.

Linda looked at him then at the women trapped inside the mirror. She wanted to free her, but could only pity her; she wished she could do something, but the powerful wizard had frightened her. She looked away then spoke quietly:

"I'm very sorry to hear that." She said.

The mirror shattered into thousands of pieces, which transformed back into a waterfall.

Raising above it the dinosaur emerged with the wizard's wife and her boyfriend captured firmly in its claws. The wizard lashed his wand:

"E eternity, e eternity." He raged.

At that moment appeared gashes of light and then the lake reinstated.

The wizard quietly walked towards a small boat before gesturing his hand for Linda to follow she obeyed; she found herself frightened and huddled beside Scott inside the boat while the wizard paddled along the lake until he arrived at a beautiful palace that was set in fine woodland.

On entering through the gates there was lots of little gnomes, leprechauns and statues of small people deposited in the gardens that moved their eyes and turned their heads, after they had all entered the palace.

Unknown to them they were alive. Miraculously the garden reverted into a city for gnomes, leprechauns, and small people who suddenly became active. There were men dressed in bright colours who wore pointed hats and were accompanied by their short, fat wives in long, dresses and head scarf's;

they watched their children play briskly in the parks and gardens swinging on swings and rocking on sea-saws.

The supermarkets, shops, schools and banks were full of citizens of the city who actively went about their business.

There were houses neatly positioned beneath the huge bushes and behind the tall trees, where lovely net curtains draped from the windows.

Gerry was a leprechaun that dug tunnels and often worked hard to support his family; he arrived home wearing a tall, green hat and beaming with happiness.

The door flung open to an aroma of vegetables and fried fish cooking on the stove.

In the small kitchen knives and folks neatly prepared on the small wooden table accompanied with vacant chairs.

Inside the lounge lying on the sofa was Ivy his wife.

"I found a pot of gold at the end of the rainbow." Gerry shouted as he barged through the door carrying a sack on his back, which he dropped when kneeling down to throw his arms around her; as she stretched her cheek for him to kiss.

"Hello, Ivy Love" He said kissing her cheek.

"Hello, Gerry." She replied.

He stood up and walked over to the table untying his bag to release mountains of gold that soon reproduced itself throughout the house. The gold was magical and kept pouring from the bag.

Ivy was amazed she had never seen so much gold.

"Close the bag!" She ordered.

Gerry tied the sack and the gold stopped reproducing. The leprechauns danced around uncontrollably.

"We're rich, were rich," they sang.

Many regions of Citizen City were on the grounds of the palace, whilst the remainder of the city was situated six feet underground. It was sheer intelligence, artistry magic and the ability to freeze at the sight of spiritual beings which made this village unique.

Melissa and Una were Gerry and Ivy's beautiful twin daughters they both attended the local comprehensive school which was in the heart of the city surrounded by beautiful, tall trees and an array of vibrant flowers.

The black board displayed formulas and calculations written by Mr. Connolly their teacher and an ambassador of the city, which Melissa and Una copied whilst seated amongst the other children dressed in grey or black trousers with white shirts. The pupil's appeard remarkably similar only gnomes and leprechauns were distinguishable. The leprechauns all wore distinguished tall, green hats and the gnome's wore big, red, woolly ones.

On finishing her day Melissa packed the last of her books whilst Una rushed through the door.

"Wait for me! I have games," She shouted to her sister who smiled and nodded back at her whilst packing her books and heading to the door.

"Melissa, could you wait a minute?" Mr. Connolly said gulping down coffee whilst peering through his glasses at her.

Melissa looked over to him:

"Mr. Connolly have I done something wrong?" She asked.

"Oh no, no, no, it's far from that, dear." He replied.

Mr. Connolly was a very scruffy gnome his shirt was never tucked into his trousers and his hair was often very greasy with strands of long hair often falling to the side revealing the baldness of his head that he often tried to disguise.

The last pupil left leaving Mr. Connolly rubbing his hands excitedly when walking over to Melissa.

"I have just been informed that your father found the pot of gold at the end of the rainbow. He came only last week asking for the formula. No doubt he will want the best schools for both you and your sister." He said.

Melissa confused by this found it hard to believe.

"My father has the pot of gold. I don't understand sir." She said still puzzled.

"Nonetheless, the swords your father wanted have arrived I know he expressed a desire for them, but there is a price." He said.

"I don't think he can afford them; were struggling with the bills at home and my school fee is well over due sir!" She informed.

"Oh no there has been no mistake your father has the pot of gold, young lady!

He has got the pot of gold." He repeated vehemently.

Melissa still found it very strange as she reviewed everything that Mr. Connolly had said before becoming only partially convinced.

"I had no idea sir. Are you sure it was my father?" She questioned.

"It's hard for you to believe, but I'm sure you will find it's very real and your father is by no doubt the wealthiest man in the village." He continued whilst returning to his desk to finish his coffee.

Gerry sat at the kitchen table whilst Ivy dished up steamed potatoes with fish that they tucked into whilst laughing and joking about recent events when Melissa and Una strolled into the house to notice the piles of gold everywhere which made Melissa realize her teacher was telling the truth.

Both girls joined their parents at the table whilst their father explained how he retrieved the gold.

"I had the formula and I knew the rainbow stopped east of the ocean, but I had to calculate it. It was Mr. Connolly's formula that I used" Gerry explained.

"Whoopee, whoopee;" the family responded.

They ate their dinners with their eyes fixed on piles of gold which beamed through the kitchen door creating excitement, joy and laughter throughout the family home.

Once the laughter had settled down Ivy remembered the gossip that she wanted to share with her husband:

"Oh wise Wesley has been the talk of the town the rumour is Lady Sarah's been having an affair with the young pauper boy that worked in the stables." She said which left Gerry shocked.

"That is ghastly news. Are you sure? He queried.

Ivy nodded.

"I don't know if there's any truth in that, but wise Wesley has the wizard genes in him. Some gnomes have claimed to see him at work. They won't be able to keep that a secret for very long." He said.

Ivy saw when Linda and Scott entered the house they intrigued her she turned to Gerry.

"I saw some people entering the palace today who were they?" She asked.

"I don't know! Maybe they were friends. I've never seen them." He said whilst the family continued munching away admiring the piles of gold.

"I will be down the bank first thing tomorrow with all that gold, our kids will go to the best school and we will have businesses throughout the whole city. I may even buy the bank." Gerry joked at which time Melissa informed her father about the conversation she had with her teacher:

"I spoke to Mr. Connolly today he said the swords are ready."

Gerry immediately stopped eating becoming excited by the news. "They have actually arrived?" He asked. Melissa nodded in response. Gerry knew of the five ancient swords, but never dreamt that one day he would be able to afford them.

They were very special because each sword had unique, magical powers that were capable of revealing the past, present, future and they were able to adjust too many tasks. if used in the correct way and guarded the owner when on dangerous missions.

"Mr. Connolly's a genius. I'll pick the swords up and reward him handsomely for his formula." He said.

In the interim time back at the palace, Wesley led Linda and Scott along the polished wooden floors though to the great hall where they saw beautiful murals hanging from walls before seating them at the elegant table dressed with fine silver.

Wesley left the room for a while. Linda and Scott discussed how evil he was after witnessing his earlier activities.

"Evil Wicked Man" Scott said.

"Be quiet, I know" Linda whispered clearly worried that Wesley would hear them.

Wesley soon arrived with his wand walking calmly towards them.

"Alcatraz, Alcatraz." He shouted his cloak opened wide as he stretched his hands up into the air.

"You will forget the events you witnessed earlier! You know nothing of my powers." He said.

This caused them to immediately collapse over the table before Wesley carried them to a large chamber where they slept.

It had been a few weeks since Linda and Scott entered the palace. Wesley cooked and cleaned for his new guest trying hard to keep them entertained, but they were bored and desperately wanted to leave. Scott was restless when he turned to his mother and said:

"I have travelled around every room of the palace and searched for an amusement, but I have not found any."

Wesley heard Scott complaining and then walked angrily towards him he had grown tired of Scott, but was becoming extremely fond of Linda.

"Let your son go to the palace lake and fill his heart with all the hidden secrets and mystique these grounds and lakes can offer." He suggested to her, but she was reluctant to leave Scott wandering around in a strange place alone.

"I will go with him!" She replied.

"He's a big lad, I'm sure he doesn't want mummy watching his every move." He said whilst Linda remained adamant to remain with her son.

"No I insist I must accompany him." She insisted.

"Then go if you so wish, but I insist you join me later for dinner just the two of us!" He demanded.

Linda had witnessed Wesley becoming extremely fond of her which left her uncomfortable because she knew they could only be friends.

"I would love to dine with you, Wesley, but I won't let Scott out of my sight for a moment. This place is unfamiliar and there have been strange encounters.

"I'm truly grateful, Wesley for all the kindness that you have shown." She said.

Wesley contained his anger directed at Scott who was becoming a big problem for him because he despised all the love Linda showed towards her son, but was desperate to pursue a lasting relationship with her, but first he had to find a way to get rid of Scott.

Linda and Scott left the palace walking through the beautiful gardens; they were unaware of Citizen City where the leprechaun's gnomes and small people lived.

Large bushes bordered the lawn and a range of vibrant flowers protruded all around the grounds.

Whilst walking beside the lake they noticed the small boat anchored to the bank which had bought them there.

As they boarded the boat Linda noticed two leprechauns carrying a strange opened box containing golden crafted swords and a large sack of gold which they guarded.

Linda smiled before seating herself beside the leprechaun; she thought it peculiar that they were there.

"Scott I think these leprechauns are coming with us." She said.

Scott studied their pleasant faces, the box and a sack of gold beside them before paddling further away from the palace grounds towards the beautiful nesting spots along the shore. Across the lake they noticed dears running freely and small birds perching from trees.

Gerry and Ivy remained silent throughout unaware that Linda and Scott would be accompanying them. He was intending to deposit the gold and try out the swords from Mr. Connolly.

Scott amused by the leprechauns watched them keenly. Gerry then blinked and sneezed "Atischoo, Atischoo" Scott was amazed he watched eagerly to see if he would sneeze again.

"Atischoo, Atischoo." He sneezed again.

Gerry's eyes opened and Scott stared curiously.

"Mum the leprechauns are alive." He shouted.

Linda looked around at the tiny leprechauns smiling at her with Gerry adjusting his hat.

"Hello there little one . . . what are you doing here?" She asked.

At that moment, Gerry used the magic from the sword to transform, Ivy and then himself and his possession to full size image.

Linda and Scott, was astonished when observing Gerry and Ivy's full size image.

"Indeed I shall go rowing! With ebony swords with handles of wood worked gold. These are no ordinary swords there are five magical sword and each have there unique functions that can reveal the present, past and future." Gerry said whilst he paddled away at immense speed using the handles of the sword; which left everyone holding on tightly.

They were cruising along the still waters when unfortunately Linda tangled her paddle with her pendant that fell into the lake and left her feeling troubled. She grew silent because this was a gift from her grandmother and she had never been without it. Ivy saw Linda's disappointment and began to comfort her.

"Oh dear, don't be sad miss." She said.

"My grandmother gave it to me. I've never been without it." Linda wept.

Gerry immediately stopped paddling, searching the sack he pulled out a pile of gold and handed it to her.

"I've loads of gold take some and buy a new one!" He insisted.

He ruffled through the sack of gold grabbing handfuls of it and giving it to Linda leaving Ivy very embarrassed.

"Gerry It's a sentimental loss dear it can't be replaced." She said before taking back the gold and putting it back into the sack.

Gerry pulled another sword from his box which he placed in the water that immediately dried up to reveal a large stone where the pendant lodged. Linda quickly retrieved her necklace and Gerry removed the sword to place it back inside the box.

The lake returned with a strange woman hovering above it.

Ivy studied the women and then blurted: "It's Lady Sarah!" She said looking very startled to why she was there. Lady Sarah, smiled at Ivy admiringly, she had no recollection of who she was, but was happy that she had recognized her.

"Don't be afraid of me! Please help me." She pleaded.

Gerry immediately went to his box then looked at Lady Sarah's sorrowful face before he replied:

"Mm, I will see."

Opening the box, a bright light beamed from the swords inside as Gerry pondered over which one to use before lifting one above his head.

"I am he the owner of the sword." He shouted.

He placed it into the lake at the same tome a ball of smoke appeared which transformed into large grey lips that smoked before uttering:

"Lady Sarah is unaware of the great wizard who cast the spell on her. It is a mammoth task to break the spell; you need to seek the book of magic and this will enable you to obtain the powers and wisdom. Living beings and a magic snake that cannot die will guard the book. Only the owner of the magic sword will have any chance of completing this mission and succeeding."

Gerry removed the sword from the lake and the lips vanished; he suddenly noticed Scott and Linda's faces trapped inside the lake which made him aware that they too were in danger.

Ivy noticed the concerned look on Gerry's face which puzzled her.

"What's wrong?" She asked, but Gerry barely responded because he was in deep thought.

"Wesley is the great wizard!" She persisted. This time Gerry nodded because she confirmed what he already knew.

"Gerry only you can break the spell . . . What will you do?" Ivy asked.

"I will go . . . I will try to help Lady Sarah." He said putting another sword into the lake causing the lips to appear once more:

"Scott and Linda are in danger the great wizard is looking to dispose of them too."

Linda and Scott, were devastated on hearing this and listened keenly to the lips said when Ivy interrupted turning to Gerry:

"Go to Mr. Connolly, he will give you advice on how to complete this mission. Mr. Connolly is the wisest gnome in the city?" She shouted excitedly.

"Calm down dear, it's vital for us to listen to what the lips are saying" Gerry replied this silenced her prior to the lips continuing.

"The serpent that cannot die guards the book of magic. Seek this book for wisdom and knowledge." The lips then faded,

Lady Sarah was shocked at what she heard.

"My husband is the great wizard . . . It should have been apparent . . . . He knew of the affair; he knows how to move mountains, but he has failed in his quest for a woman's love! He will destroy any woman whom refuses to love him . . . He is a very evil man." She alleged as everyone pitied her before she too began to fade.

"Can I not be saved?" She asked.

"I will try!" Gerry said before she completely vanished.

Gerry turned his attention to Linda whose reflection he saw in the lake.

"Oh dear, Oh dear, you're destined for the same fate. Wesley has fallen for you too, but you will fail to love him and become his victim. He despises Scott who is in danger." He warned, leaving Linda and Scott extremely worried.

"What are we to do?" Linda asked.

Again he was in deep thought that made him aware of the instructions that the lips had given him. He sat quietly reviewing everything before speaking:

"Wesley has got a book of magic spells . . . which must be retrieved to reverse the spell, but first the knowledge and the power must be sought. Linda you must return to the palace and charm him to buy us time. We will need to get you and Scott away from that place, but we must be careful because he is a very powerful wizard. This mission will be hopeless unless I gain the wisdom and power to defeat him," he said.

Gerry arrived at Mr. Connolly house for the master plan . . . Mr. Connolly was very intrigued by what he said and knew he had a difficult task ahead of him.

"Gerry why is it I did not know about this. Lady Sarah is a very kind woman! When did this happen?" Mr. Connolly asked whilst having a drink with Gerry.

"I don't know." Gerry replied.

"'I' must go to the lake and speak to Lady Sarah at once!" Mr. Connolly insisted as he rushed over to a cupboard to retrieve his coat.

Mr. Connolly and Gerry returned to the lake to discover that Gerry had forgotten his magic sword.

"The sword I do not have them."

"Do not worry! I can summon her to appear." Mr. Connolly said.

"Lady Sarah I command your presence." He shouted and Lady Sarah immediately appeared.

"Oh, Lady Sarah I'm sorry to hear of your misfortunes. I have watched and admired your kind works for many years" Mr. Connolly said.

"Oh thank you both very much for coming" she smiled warmly and then continued.

"I wish you prosperous and healthy lives. I have been called and I have come." She said.

"It is dreadful what has happened. Your husband is the evil wizard that puts this evil spell on you!" Mr. Connolly said whilst Lady Sarah nodded in agreement.

"I have witnessed magical things by him, but was foolish never to question anything. A bird lay lifeless before him . . . . Wesley said his words of magic and the bird arose." She said.

Mr. Connolly realized the depth of Wesley's powers then questioned her further.

"How many chambers are there in the palace?" He asked.

"There are many chambers there, but in the tower there is a secret chamber that is always locked." She informed.

Mr. Connolly pressed her further about the locked chamber: "Where is the key?" He asked.

"The key is kept in a locked chess under his bed or it is carried on his key ring.

Mr. Connolly knew that the secret chamber was the most likely place to find the book of magic spells and they would need to retrieve the key. He also knew it would be a mammoth task ahead of them because. Wesley was a very powerful and wise.

He knew that Gerry would need to acquire the knowledge and powers to defeat such a force and he would need to venture on this quest immediately.

CHAPTER 5

The Mission

Gerry had been sailing for days armed with the magic sword and the formulas that Mr. Connolly composed. He used his compass to locate his position then carefully calculate the route.

He toiled without ceasing by day and night by the third day he arrived at the island that contained the knowledge and power he sought. He stood on the island calculating the spot before he started digging.

Gerry stopped digging when a huge green snake suddenly became visible. The serpent up stretched and towered above him. He stepped back when the snake hissed at him and pulled out one of the swords.

"Give me the power to defeat the serpent." He ordered. The sword immediately transformed into a powerful golden sword which he lashed at the serpent that immediately dissected and lay before him; he continued digging then stepped back when an army of enormous black scorpions emerged; grabbing his shovel he battered them, but more appeared jumping at him which he tried to fend off before reaching for his sword. He started to remember the warning about the box as he raised the sword above his head:

"Around the iron box snakes and scorpions twined." He knew they were living, moving creatures ready to kill anyone who dared to go near the box. Raising the sword higher above his head he shouted to the skies: "I am he the owner of the magic sword. Be gone I demand"

All the insects vanished which enabled him to continue digging and then more identical snakes appeared.

"I am the owner of the sword be gone!" He demanded again, but it was useless the sword became powerless the deeper he dug.

He continued to slay the snakes as they hissed and snarled at him eventually defeating them one by one.

Overwhelmed on realizing he had found the magic box he lifted it out of the sand and opened it; there inside was the book of magic, when he reached for it a huge serpent appeared. Gerry lashed off the serpent's head and immediately the serpent joined together and made ready to stop Gerry from reaching the book. Once again he beheaded the snake and tossed the head into the sea. Yet again the serpent's head flew to the body and the reptile was alive protecting the book.

Gerry could not slay the serpents so he thought of a cunning plan. So once more he struck off its head, but before the head and body could come together he put rocks on each part, so when they tried to join they could not do so as there were rocks between them and the serpent that could not die lay helpless in two pieces.

Gerry opened the large, dusty, old book that ejected a heavy presence of moving light that entered him. He had acquired the wisdom and powers to retract the spell on Lady Sarah and overcome the removal of wise Wesley.

Meanwhile at the palace, Linda wined and dined Wesley; she had convinced him that she loved him and he agreed to celebrate their engagement by throwing a glamorous party.

Mr. Connolly used magic to transform the residents of Citizen Cities into wealthy people from nearby towns in order for them to gain entry to the banquet; on entering Linda and Scott greeted them by winking and smiling approvingly.

Wesley was busy entertaining the other guest whilst Linda sneaked Gerry to the room to retrieve the key.

Cobwebs accompanied with a cold and airy atmosphere was present on Gerry entered the secret chamber there were many different size bottles containing colourful liquids and a huge selection of spell books on the shelves. There was also a large wooden table with a small cage situated in the middle of the room.

He immediately searched through the books, hoping to find the book of magic spells so he could retract the spell on Lady Sarah. He had been searching for a while, but was unable to find the book; just as he had given up hope and decided to stop searching he noticed a large container hidden beneath the shelves.

He sat at the table to open it retrieving a huge, dusty book when he wiped away the dust he was left puzzled to why there was no title. He opened the book to find a picture of three witches sitting around a cauldron; he continued to study the picture then noticed items appearing that were familiar to him; there were shelves with spell books and portions and a large table with a man reading a book. He quickly closed the book when grasping it was the secret chamber and himself present inside the book.

Then to his dismay the three witches appeared just as they were in the book around a cauldron directly in front of him; he stared at them in disbelief as they stirred the contents in the pot ahead of walking towards him.

"You opened the book!" They repeated.

Gerry remained shocked and stunned by them, but stood his ground.

"I'm searching for the book of magic spells to retract a spell" He said.

"You have found it!" One of the witches announced pointing at the closed book on the table before him.

The book mystified him, he did not envisage there to be real time witches inside the book.

"I command you to tell me how to retract the spell on Lady Sarah." He said.

The witches returned to the cauldron and one witch continued to stir it.

"We can retract the spell if you wish" another witch said.

Gerry was pleased that the witches could help him until the witch stopped stirring and said:

"There is one condition."

"What's the condition?" He asked.

"There is a test that you must do." The witch continued.

Gerry was eager to know what this test was and walked over to them, but was mortified to discover arms and legs were simmering in the cauldron.

They giggled and laughed at Gerry's mortified face then all the witches laughed out as they rubbed their hands: "Citizen City is at stake, if your powers are a fake, we will test to see if you are weak, then we' well give the spell you seek." They all recited together.

Gerry did not want to continue with the quest, but he kept seeing Lady Sarah's face inside his head.

"What must I do?" He asked.

"Turn the page! Turn the page!" They said before disappearing."

Gerry opened the book again where the witches remained huddled beside the cauldron, but this time he did not see himself around the table. He was about to turn the next page when he stopped to grab the box containing his swords then proceeded to turn the page.

"There were enormous four legged beasts that looked fierce and gruesome, they were huge like elephants and strong like an ox with heads and torso formed from man; the beast guarded the trees that had shields beside them belonging to the many conquerors that had challenged, but failed.

There in the mist of the beast's territory stood a man with a box; the beast sniffed around completely unaware of the presence of a challenger. Gerry was unaware that many conquerors had sacrificed their cities becoming victims of the witch's cauldron. At the same time Gerry continued to read the book which read:

"It is the bark of the tree you seek that's the magic ingredient needed to retract the spell on Lady Sarah."

Great magicians had seconded the beast to guard the tree which allowed their spells never to be broken more important to safeguard their title as the most powerful in the kingdom.

Gerry continued to read the book discovering he was the man who had come to challenge the beast; he turned over the page to see pictures of him-self standing beneath a gigantic toadstool opening the box to retrieve his sword.

Pulling a sword trimmed with fine gold that shone brightly, he held it above his head.

"I am the owner of the sword." He shouted before confronting the beast who then tried to capture him with his large, furry hands. Gerry had escaped the beast by a whisker and continued to lash out at him with his sword; the beast looked down to see Gerry attacking him then picked him up and threw him, causing him to lose his sword before landing on a large mushroom; he bounced off to roll under the toadstool for refuge. The beast roared before attacking the toadstool.

Then more beasts appeared gathering around the toadstool roaring fiercely. Again the beast attacked the toadstool this time Gerry was exposed and every beast ran at him snarling their teeth as they tried to slay him. He ran under another toadstool, but the beasts scented him out and injured him whilst attacking the large mushroom. Injured and rolling on the floor he reached for a shield. The shield of conquerors that had failed the quest, which he used to shield him from the beast.

He ran frantically to the wooden box then he retrieved another sword which he held to the skies.

"I command you to transform these beasts to babies." He shouted and immediately young beast played blissfully through the trees whilst Gerry scraped the bark with his sword.

Gerry closed the book to discover the witches immediately appeared adding the bark to the cauldron, along with the coloured liquids they had taken from the shelves. Gerry watched on mystified as the witches continued to stir the cauldron that bubbled over whilst reciting a spell.

"Cook and stir what's in the pot . . . Until it bubbles to the top . . . The wicked wizard's spell will wear . . . when the substance is crystal clear."

The sound of the alarms rang throughout the whole palace when Wesley realized that somebody had entered his secret chamber; he raced up the stairs, his cloak became larger on him reaching the chamber door; he was reduced to a small hamster trapped in his cape.

Gerry knew exactly whom he was when throwing the cape off the hamster before picking him up by his tail and placing him in the empty cage; he locked the door and hung a sign which read, "Never open this door!"

The palace doorbell rang loudly. Mr. Connolly answered it outside dripping wet was, Lady Sarah and her friend. Mr. Connolly immediately rushed to her flinging his arms around her ahead of leading them through to the banquet, where they were welcomed by praising, singing and joyful sounds as everyone celebrated her safe return.

Everyone danced with joy when Gerry came down the huge spiral stairs to reassure everyone that wicked and evil Wesley was no longer a threat to anyone.

They continued to enjoy themselves until Mr. Connolly approached Linda and Scott to inform them it was time for them to leave:

"Linda, you must leave now! This is not the place for people who suddenly arrive. People can stay here for many years, before they decide to board the train and continue their journey. The residents that are born here are the gnomes, leprechauns, and small people. It can take centuries for some spiritual beings to realize they must move on.

Your train will be arriving soon. You have a mission ahead of you . . . I wish you well, be careful." He said.

Linda and Scott were grateful as they hugged and kissed everyone before leaving for pastures new.

Linda held Scott's hand and hurriedly walked towards the building far in the distance.

"That must be the station! Linda thought as she viewed the huge trees, beautiful flowers and plants that surrounded it. Her thoughts soon drifted to Emily who was home alone.

"We need to get back home for Emily . . . She will be worried about us." She said as Scott nodded in agreement.

"You will need to be brave this place can get very dangerous and we do not know when those bees may return." She warned whilst they both continued towards the building.

Scott listened keenly to what his mother said ahead of becoming astounded by the large stalks from different types of flowers towering above them nodding and whispering as they hurried along.

Linda guarded Scott because she had never encountered talking flowers.

"We won't hurt him." They shouted down to her.

Linda and Scott looked up in amusement at the army of flowers that had suddenly come into bloom.

"You must not go over to that building because you will be captured." Another flower warned as the petals formed lips.

Unexpectedly the other flowers agreed by nodding their petals and whispering, whilst marching along with Linda and Scott.

Linda realized the beautiful flowers were harmless as they seem to be warning them about the dangers that lay ahead.

"We are trying to get to the station over there." Linda explained before pointing to the station.

A flower then spoke in a squeaky voice as its petals formed into lips.

"You must let us help you . . . You will be safe once you reach the station." A high-pitched voice echoed from the petals that had formed lips.

Linda was aware that the station was safe, but was still confused about the dangers that the flowers warned about.

"What dangers do we need protecting from?" She asked the flowers after they stopped marching and turned to leave her.

"The birds they are vicious, they will harm you." It was at that time purple-feathered birds flew over them then disappeared into the clouds.

Linda continued walking towards the station when she noticed the purple-feathered creatures paroling the entrance then gliding towards her.

The flowers immediately grew taller as they joined together to form a solid bed.

The huge birds flapped angrily then squawked to alert the other birds, who immediately arrived to hover over the flower beds, aware the flowers were shielding them as they remained frightened beneath the bed of flowers as the flying creatures continued to squawk at the flowers.

Gathering speed the stalks transformed to legs that ran with Linda and Scott towards the building as the birds violently destroyed the flowerbeds leaving Linda and Scott in full view of the gigantic flying creatures.

"Run, Scott run!" Linda shouted.

They both raced towards the building whilst two flying creatures flew at them before the flowers bloomed instantly to shield them.

A frightened and shocked Linda cuddled Scott as they sat imprisoned between the stems which isolated them from the birds.

The huge reptiles looked around frantically before growing tired of waiting and flew away; the flowerbeds shrunk back to a minimal size to reveal a frightened and shocked Linda and Scott that lay flat out on the fields.

"It's safe to go now! The birds have gone." A flower said.

They stood up to thank the flowers and then ran towards the station entrance.

CHAPTER 6

The Communication Room

The presence of big black iron gates appeared before them, above the word "Station"

The gates prized open by Linda who held Scott's hand and slowly walked up the shiny, ivory staircase that led to large, white wooden door. Pushing open the door revealed a waiting room.

There they stood stunned by the beautiful shiny, white, marble floor with red, ivory benches mounted on the walls. Above hanging from the tall, white ceiling was an information board dressed with golden borders.

Ahead of them was a small, white door with a big, red doorknob with thick, white mist coming through the gaps around the frame.

Suddenly the information board blinked continuously before displaying the train destinations. Linda pondered at the board that read: Nowhere, Cloudland, Red Fire and Earth. She held Scott's hand tighter and continued to walk through the waiting room amazed by the large bay window with 'Ticket Hall' written above. She walked over and peeped at electrical servers, large transformers and other electrical equipment that was unrecognizable to her; positioned neatly on the wall opposite there was a large clock with large, golden numbers set in a crystal face ticking and beneath it were many compact computer workstations.

Then she noticed a brass bell beside her attached to a computer inside the ticket hall.

She pushed the bell that let of a loud audible sound which echoed throughout the waiting room; simultaneously the computers consecutively switched on.

Linda and Scott stood bemused watching as the keyboards started to depress themselves, causing monitors to display codes and formulas which meant nothing to them.

Then the hatch dispatched tickets, letters and small objects. Linda immediately picked up a card with a message addressed.

"We know you'll be back soon." The message read. She picked up another card with another message addressed before she continued to read as many messages as she could.

This was very strange for her the messages had been sent by people she knew very well whilst others were not familiar. She picked up a small, white, fluffy teddy bear with a message attached.

"I hope you pull through, love and kisses signed Emily with a kiss." She held the teddy close to her heart, but it vanished; she knew her daughter had sent it.

Linda was aware that something had happened that was the reason for the messages. Scott continued to search for more messages "I'm so sorry x Jill," "We miss you both "were a few of the messages Scott read.

Linda still confused about exactly what was happening she pondered to find clarification about what was going on.

"That message was from Emily; there are messages from people we know; they are all wishing us well!" She said.

Linda knew this was not an ordinary ticket hall, but a kind of communications port that was capable of connecting with people that she knew. Was it also possible that it could communicate with the other destinations on the board? She wondered.

They continued to read the messages dropping through the hatch as quickly as she read them they vanished. She then turned to Scott:

"There was a message from Emily . . . There all messages for us Scott! Something must have happened to us!" She said as she searched for clarification of the bizarreness that they were encountering.

Scott listened keenly as he slowly digested what his mother had said.

The ticket hall suddenly went quiet, when the machines stopped. The only sound was the ticking of the large clock and then the hatch flapped open to post five, large golden tickets.

Each ticket had a name in bold, gold letters that read: Jason, Charlie, Linda, Scott and Luck beneath the names read "Take Me."

Linda was bewildered by the names on the tickets as she put them in her bag ahead of walking towards the door with the red knob.

Thick, cloudy mist filled the waiting room when Linda pulled open the door to reveal a platform.

She held Scott's hand tightly when stepping out onto the platform, only to step back quickly inside, slamming the door shut on hearing a loud banging coming from the tracks.

"We are not alone son!" She whispered.

"Do not be afraid! That person may be able to help us." Scott told her.

"Person . . . Linda responded. It could be anything out there, Scott!" She shouted aware of the dangers that surrounded them; she remembered the pigeon sized bees and the large birds; she knew she had to put on a brave face because she did not want Scott to think she was a coward, but she was frightened of the strange place. She hated all that she had witnessed. The fear that came over her made Scott aware that his mum was not as brave as he had first thought.

"Something is out there!" She whispered again whilst the panic and weakness took control of her, as she broke down on the white marble floor.

"I'm frightened Scott . . . I don't know if I can stand this place for a minute longer." She cried.

Scott knew he would have to take control. Slowly he pulled open the door the mist filled the waiting room whilst they stepped onto the platform. Scott grabbed his mother's hand before disappearing into the mist.

The noise got louder on the sudden emergence of a figure in the mist. Linda backed away whilst staring at the man who wore a blue baseball cap, bright, orange overall and had a disfigured face.

The man unaware of Linda chipped away at a bolt holding two rails together.

The chipping stopped when the man turned around to notice them. "Linda Harris?" He asked.

"Yes!" She answered puzzled to whom this man was that spoke with a deep Scottish accent.

She stared hard at the face that looked familiar but was unrecognizable to her. Jumping onto the platform he smiled at Scott. "And who is this wee lad?" He asked.

Linda smiled politely as the man appeared more visible to her when he came out of the mist.

"Scott." She responded to the big strapping man with a plaited, goatee beard as he removed his blue cap to expose his curly, black and grey hair. He looked fierce with the disfigurement leaving Linda struggling to recognise him and then she immediately flung her arms around him. It was Charlie! The gentle giant she had spent many hot, sunny days with maintaining the railway signalling systems.

"Oh I'm so glad to see you, Charlie . . . I thought there was no one else here, but us then I heard banging and I didn't know what to expect." She explained.

Scott looked on with relief he was happy his mother's confidence had returned before Linda introduced him properly.

"Scott I want you to meet Charlie he is my boss at work. He's taught me everything I know about the railways, when he took me under his wings I had just left school." Linda said as Charlie smiled at Scott and then shook his hand vigorously.

"Hello lad, please to meet you." He said before pointing at the point machine positioned on the side of the track "Your mother spends hours fixing those." He said.

Scott bewildered with fingers pointed towards it then questioned. "What is it?"

"It's a point machine used to move the trains to different tracks. Your mum's a professional; she knows all about the railways."

He continued whilst admiring Linda's intelligence and flair which were prominent features in her characteristics. She tried hard to maintain her youthful, stylish image, but sometimes it was difficult as she spent most of her time maintaining greasy, dirty equipment and her work often involved climbing the stanchions to repair signals.

Being the only women in her department sometimes became too much when her male counterparts often reminded her of what a women's role was. Nonetheless she was a very determined, young woman and always happy to prove she was equal or better than her male competitors.

Linda was achieving her goals at work and it came as no surprised when rewarded with promotion. She had demonstrated in her interview that she was the best candidate for promotion despite the heavy competition.

Charlie smiled at her as he remembered this happy, young woman that had brought so much sunshine and joy to his work. It was not long before his thoughts were interrupted. Linda expressed sorrow. She pitied him when she stared back at a disfigured face covered in cuts and bruising. This was very different from the tall, handsome man she admired.

Charlie embarrassed by his disfigurement often had spells of deep thought when reminded of it.

It was a hot, sunny day when Charlie was out working on the track, whilst being protected from trains by a lookout who alerted him of the presents of a train:

"Charlie!" The lookout shouted, but he continued hammering away at the bolts on the track as the driver of the May pen expresses blew his horn and waved his hands vigorously in his cabin when Charlie looked up he could only see the train darting down on him.

The locomotive slowly came to a halt. Charlie's blue hat blew along the track.

Linda noticed the despair and sadness that came over him and asked: "What's wrong?"

Charlie collected his thoughts then answered: "Something happened to me!" Linda waited for him to continue, but he stared in silence which caused her to drift into thoughts about events when she was last at work.

There was a notice board filled with information about weekend working, safety bulletin and a picture of Charlie attached to a notice that read "Railway man seriously injured."

Below the notice were tables, there was an old, white fridge accompanied by a gas cooker with a kettle whistling on it that Linda used to pour boiling water into cups.

The tea handed to her friends, as they chatted until the boss arrived. "There was a serious accident and it resulted in one of our staff, Charlie Johnson critical in hospital." The supervisor announced.

Linda's thoughts were constantly with Charlie, as she sat chatting about him with her workmates. "Charlie of all people . . . he was the most experience man here . . . he taught me all I knew" she said retracting her thoughts to find herself looking at Charlie's disfigurement which led to her asking the dreaded question. "Are we dead Charlie?"

Charlie avoided the answer as he jumped back onto the tracks and continued to chip away at the rusty bolts.

"Critical that's all they said." Linda shouted to him as she tried to make sense of everything.

Charlie looked up at her becoming concerned because her hands trembled with fear when she covered her mouth. He stopped, but he was to beside himself to know how to comfort her because he too was struggling with coming to terms with everything that had happened.

"What happened to you, Linda?" He asked.

The paramedics entered her mind as she remembered the accident. She continued with her thoughts then stared at Charlie before she quietly spoke "All I remember was Scott and I were on our way to the match." She stopped as her softly spoken voice began to relive terrible moments encountered which left her shaking.

Charlie's thoughts were with her; how could she end up in a place like this? It must be very stressful for her. She had substituted her happy go lucky smile for a worried look and all her bravery had disappeared leaving a timid frightened woman. Charlie wished he could do more for her, but knew he was unstable and worried about what would become of him then a terrible thought came into his mind . . . They may never return to their lives.

Linda was in deep thought, when a disturbing look compelled her face: "Wait a minute; no it can't be." She said looking at him confusingly.

"How long have you been here, Charlie?" She asked. Charlie shook his head.

"I don't know. I have lost all track of time." He said.

Visions of Linda's work entered her thoughts again as she remembered all the workers who had collected money and bought a card for Charlie.

"I don't think you made it, Charlie!" She said with a stern voice.

"You don't think I made it." He repeated.

Linda nodded; she waited for an angry response from him, but was pleasantly surprised when he responded. "That's good!" He shouted joyfully.

Linda looked puzzled, when he wiped away tears from his eyes and his sadness immediately turned to joy before he spoke again.

"My dear child you have just answered my question! This was immensely frightful.

This is the end! We are finished were the thoughts in my mind, but then you said critical before, now you say you do not think I made it. You are not sure! That spells hope! Cloudland's not the only place on that board the train can take you right back to Earth."

Charlie was convinced he had figured out a portion of the mystery that surrounded them leaving Linda happy for him.

"Charlie of all the people I could meet I wonder why I bumped into you?" She asked.

"There are four places we can go now that's Nowhere, Cloudland, Red Fire and Earth. You didn't see the board inside?" He asked as Linda and Scott nodded simultaneously.

Our destiny is in our own hands . . . We have hope child of returning to our lives!

I have a question for you, Linda where are you going?"

She remained silent as she looked at him; he had come alive with the belief he could return to Earth.

"I'm heading home, I'm going home to my Emily, who will be waiting for us." She responded leaving Charlie smiling approvingly. "I'm going back to my life on Earth! I'm not done with that life yet." He said.

CHAPTER 7

The Football Match

It was decided that they would all to go back to the waiting room to see when the next train would arrive. Scott sat on the red, ivory benches watching the information board when miraculously it flickered then showed interference ahead of Scott appearing on screen in his football kit.

Amazed by this they all gathered round to watch as the match got underway.

"Look mum my team." Scott shouted anxiously.

The two teams battled to book their place in the final amongst banners which read "Manley Park V Tamed Tigers" displayed around the stadium. Flyers and team sheets were fastened tightly in the hands of parents and family gathered around the side of the football pitch hollowing and shouting. Manley Park was dressed in black with bright, yellow spots and the tamed tigers wore bright, blue shirts with tigers printed on them.

Waiting for the half time whistle, Harry the manager praised his young charges for putting in a good half time performance. Scott's attention was taken away from the match when a young boy approached Harry with his father, aware of the young boy he was not happy with his antics on or off the playing field.

"Mum, that's Tommy Jenkins the boy who's trying to take my place in the team!" He shouted.

Linda watched the oversized, bald headed man who was the bearer of devastating news as the board zoomed in on the conversation he was having with Harry.

"We were delayed getting here today, Harry. Tommy was very disappointed because he knew he would have got his chance to play today." Harry continued to watch the game keenly.

"Scott Harris and his mother were involved in an accident today . . . I have been told that they are critical." Harry stopped watching the game: "Are you sure?" He asked.

Mr. Jenkins nodded leaving Harry very disturbed by the news.

Tired legs came to a halt when the half time whistle blew and the team walked off the pitch.

It became apparent the screen was showing the match that Linda and Scott were on their way too. It also made them became aware of what had happened.

After hearing the news Harry felt he needed to cancel the match, but after a meeting with all the parents they all agreed they would continue with the game. Harry addressed the team, before sending them onto the pitch.

"Give this game everything; give it your all! Do it for Scott." He screamed at them.

"The young boys threw their fist in the air as they shouted: "Yeah." Scott wouldn't want us to lose." They said.

The second half started with both teams having equal possession of the ball they battled all the time; there were shots from both sides that flew over the cross bar, hit the side netting or went just wide of the goal post; it was nail biting action.

Scott could not sit still on the bench every time he moved the screen flickered.

The goalkeeper pulled off good saves ahead of the Manley Park striker going down in the box resulting in a penalty; the strike had put Manley Park a goal up. Scott cheered and threw his arm into the air; he jumped off the bench causing the board to go completely blank.

Linda clapped and jumped excitedly after the goal. "Sit down quick!" She said to Scott then waited for the screen to return.

The game continued with excitement until the final whistle blew. Manley Park had beaten Tamed Tiger by one goal. Everyone cheered, but their thoughts were all with the missing team member and the captain of the team Scott Harris.

The screen was now in fast forward mode before displaying, Harry and the team arriving at the hospital where Emily met them. She was thrilled to see them as she explained to Harry that Scott and her mother had been involved in a collision:

"Both my mum and Scott had fallen into a coma and doctors have said its fifty, fifty. Thankfully there was no damage to the brain so if they come through its unlikely that there will be any brain damage."

Emily asked the team to sing a song for Scott for her to record on her phone. She hoped it would help to bring him back. The boys were extremely saddened to learn of Scott's misfortunes which inspired them all to sing.

"Will we win or lose? What-ever will be, will be . . . We hope it's a victory."

At the same time Scott sat on the bench and sang along with them.

"The future's not ours to see hope it's a five—nil, victory, victory." They shouted.

They continued to watch the screen and saw when the manager and teammates left. Harry returned a short time after and spoke with Emily.

"If there is anything I can do, Emily you only have to ask. Scott is a fighter he will be back with the boys . . . I know he will!"

Scott stood up and looked at his mum, he had become very emotional about what had happened. He turned and said: "I want to go home!" Then he sat back down.

Linda gave him a cuddle before reassuring him. "We will be home soon." She said.

Meanwhile, Emily thanked Harry for all the support before he left.

The screen fast forward and they all continued to watch keenly.

Nanny White, Emily's grandmother would be arriving to care for her, but she would not be comming until tomorrow. The doctors were reluctant to send Emily home alone. Her neighbour had come to collect her and assured the doctors, that she would be taking care of her until her grandmother arrived.

A shocked and frightened Emily arrived home with Edna, a petite, middle aged lady from Ireland that spoke with a strong Irish accent. She was also deeply religious; people found her aggressive and controlling, but Emily had grown up with her neighbour who was like an adopted grandmother to her.

A tearful and exhausted Emily lay on the sofa in the living room. Edna was brewing an old Irish recipe. Edna's hot, Irish whisky toddy bubbled in the saucepan which she poured into a cup, before entering the living room to find Emily with her face in a pillow whilst crouched and crying.

Edna felt sorry for her; placing the cup on the table she turned towards her snatching the pillow to notice the redness of her face and the sadness in her eyes.

"Come on, young girl that's not going to help you!" Edna said as she fixed the pillows and demanded Emily sit up before handing her, her brew.

"Hot Toddy, girl that's what I'm giving you. You need energy and strength." Edna said.

Emily slowly took the cup from her whilst trying to wipe her tear. Edna immediately took the cup back and handed her a tissue.

"Blow your nose, baby girl"; she demanded.

Emily tried to wipe her face with the tissue whilst Edna rested the hot toddy on a small table and took the tissue from her to wipe her face, but the tears kept coming.

"I've already said; I don't want to see no more tears girl!" Edna demanded.

She wiped away tears upon tears and told her to drink the brew. Emily sipped the brew and it made her cough. Edna waited for the coughing to stop.

"Another sip . . . One more, that's the way girl; your mother wouldn't like to know that you were not looking after yourself." She said.

Emily smiled she knew Edna always cheered her up however depressed she may be feeling.

"When your mother comes home and your brother too, you show them how brave and how grown up you had to be whilst they were gone." She continued.

Edna spoke as if they had gone on a vacation. Emily had terrible thoughts of them not returning. "What if they're not coming back? What will happen then?" She asked.

"Then, you will need to save some tears for when you bury them! But you won't be doing that for a long while so you don't have to worry!"

Emily became upset she could not bear to think of her mother and brother dead.

"If the good lord wanted to take them away don't you think he would have; he hasn't taken them yet my child that's why they are still with us?" We all need to pray he'll bring them right back home!" She said grabbing the empty cup from Emily's hand and placing it on the table.

"Now put your hands together whenever you're feeling down and alone you remember you're never alone the good lord is with you each step of the way; come on child put your hands together!" Emily put her hands together.

"Now pray girl every day and night you pray!" Edna said as she put her hands together and prayed with her.

Scott was feeling sad he was missing Emily he jumped off the bench and walked over to Linda for a hug.

Linda felt sad to learn that Emily was so sad she was grateful to Edna for taking good care of her.

Scott was happy that his team had won the match, but was sad that they had to play without him.

Charlie seated himself on the red, ivory bench and the board displayed a middle age woman dressed in a long, black coat with a blue, woolly hat, her face was pale, but for the redness of her eyes from crying. Charlie's wife was unrecognizable to him because he had never witnessed her so grief stricken. "Charlie, is that your wife?" Linda asked.

Charlie nodded then watched his wife who looked sad as she clutched her bible, whilst sitting by his bedside then she wept when reading from it. This saddened him he felt angry that his wife was in so much pain.

The screen turned off on Charlie leaving the bench.

A warm hug was all that Linda could offer him she hoped it would bring some comfort.

Charlie desperately wanted to be with his wife. He walked around the waiting room before kicking the ticket hall window, then he tried to enter the communication room he too believed that this room had a strong link with Earth; he bashed at the window again when that failed Charlie reached for his sledgehammer that he had been using to fix the bolt on the track.

"No Charlie!" Linda screamed, as he fiercely struck the window that shattered; at the same time the clock began to spin backwards, it spun around so quickly Linda and Scott could no longer look at it.

Charlie's eyes fixed to the clock, almost as if time was capturing him he shielded himself, but the window sucked him through and then amazingly fixed itself.

Charlie spun around on the floor whilst Linda and Scott watched on in horror.

"Charlie, Charlie can you hear me?" Linda, screamed whilst banging on the window, but there was no response from him. The clock had stopped spinning and then it chimed six times.

CHAPTER 8

The Purple Pearl

William Thomas stood with is a telescope at the crow's nest of the Purple Pearl, which was a three mast, square-rigged ship with a bowsprit that shadowed on the horizon. Seating him-self at the table drinking whiskey, he drew the ship he had just sighted.

He constructed on the paper three parts the lower mast, a top mast, top gallant mast and the bowsprit concluded the final drawing before he went down to the lower decks to address his fellow pirates, who stopped what they were doing and listened.

"It's been a hungry and tiresome journey, but good news the merchant ships been sighted. I can't tell you if it's a profit or barely to keep food in our stomach" William said.

The pirates groaned when they learned that this ship could not be for profit. They had been sailing for days avoiding the naval ships patrolling the sea, these ships filled with well-fed men that were armed and ready for combat.

Marcus Langley was a much-respected pirate who worked hand in hand with William. He stood up to silence the pirates. "It's time to prepare for battle; get the cannon's and gun's ready!" Marcus ordered. All pirates jumped up to prepare for battle with the intended target; they prepared the cannons and deposited small boats ashore armed with guns and armour then sailed towards the merchant ships.

William and Marcus were sure they could take over the merchant ship They constructed a plan which involved taking down the pirate flag and replacing it with a red flag this was a tactic often used to disguise that they were pirate.

Many pirates were worried about going to battle which made them time-lessly question Marcus about the operation as they sailed closer towards the intended target. "Am I going to live?" One crewmember shouted.

"You will die, if we don't get that capture; your next meal could be on that ship?" Marcus said before throwing the pirates overboard. "My fortune's on that ship! He shouted as the frightened pirate swarm towards the small boards before scrambling inside.

"I will be decapitated!" He shouted back to Marcus who laughed loudly and continued to throw the small boats into the sea.

The small boats arrived at the merchant ship whilst William and Marcus continued to discuss how they would capture the vessel in the hope that it would surrender.

Many pirates boarded the stern of the merchant ship battling for hours before capturing crewmembers. William changed the flag back to the pirate flag and then fired shots to force the merchant ship to surrender. The undersized merchant ship was aware that pirates were about to capture them, but they continued to battle until the captain of the merchant ship discovered that the warning shots fired by the pirates had damaged his sail.

He turned to one of his sailors, who were in combat with a pirate at the time. The clamour of swords clashed as each pirate dodged being attacked by jumping on the deck and then onto the sails.

"They have damaged the sail!" The captain shouted to the sailor that was hanging from it.

"Fight on Captain! We can't let them take us." The sailor said as he continued to lash his sword at the pirate.

"We haven't enough crew or ammunition. I don't know how many of them are still on the pirate ship." The captain shouted back to him.

The Purple Pearl sailed towards the target with pirates throwing hooks then boarding the bow to attack the merchant ships crew. The battle was fierce resulting in many pirates and crewmembers slain this resulted in more pirates sent to the merchant ships, but they were spotted by the intended target that fired shots, which resulted in the small boats capsizing. The pirates fired more cannons targeting specific areas of the merchant ship which allowed more pirates to occupy the target brandishing guns and swords.

The remaining pirates positioned themselves around the Purple Pearl yelling and showing their weapons this was a last attempt to get the merchant ship to surrender.

William Thomas had boarded the merchant ship and revealed his identity to the captain.

"William Thomas, the meanest pirate of the Caribbean sea" He announced.

At this point the captain of the merchant ship surrendered. William pulled out his gun and shot him.

"We have captured the ship!" William shouted to signal to the pirates that they had conquered the ship; they all began to rummage for valuables and cargo.

They were overwhelmed with the prize there were silver, gold coins, guns and ammunition, there was also plenty of good food and whiskey for them to feast and party.

The thunderstorms parted the sky around the Caribbean Sea as wild waves lashed through the decks of Stone Harbour.

The pirates prepared the rigging at the same time anchors were thrown overboard as the "Purple Pearl" pulled into Stone Harbour with its flag displaying the skeleton head with chilling teeth and four bones, which blew freely in the wind. Attached to the ship was the hijacked merchant ship.

William Thomas sat drinking whiskey and finishing playing cards with Marcus as they entertained women and fellow pirates.

"I had three of them surrounding me with gun's and chains. I thought I was a goner then the sky turned black and I see the one with the chain looks up at that moment I grabbed the chains from him lashing out at each of them, they dropped their gun's and I shot all three." He boasted and laughed wildly.

William was a sailor and a soldier who served under the British Crown. When celebrating a large sea robbery, they often used the harbour to dispatch all the treasure that they acquired. They allowed some passengers and crewmembers from the merchant ship to work on the Purple Pearl, others were freed and many crewmembers were enslaved and forced to work in appalling conditions.

William was heavily concentrating on the card game he was playing when Marcus turned to him: "I have found the perfect guard for the ritual tomorrow." William placed the cards on the table to acknowledge him.

Staring back at, William was a mean pirate with a patch over his left eye who had been a slave on a merchant ship; he held a grudge towards the merchant ship crew, because the crew staff had treated him badly.

He was a fearless, unpredictable pirate who made the rest of pirates shudder when he spoke. He enjoyed being a pirate and spent most of his time drunk or raging.

William was pleased that Marcus had found a good guard he nodded to signal his approval.

"Bring the guard!" William ordered before his stern face suddenly transformed back into a smile, as he continued to deal the cards.

"I've yet to find a pirate, who can beat me at this game." He laughed addressing the fellow pirates as they continued to brawl whilst preparing to play cards.

Meanwhile on the bottom decks the captives were cleaning and maintaining the ship when a captive ambushed by Marcus was taken to the higher deck.

The tobacco smoke polluted the topmast and the smell of alcohol was prominent throughout the deck when the door flung open.

The pirates stopped brawling as Marcus threw the prisoner across the floor pleading for his life.

The pirates all gathered snarling and jeering around him with their evil faces.

William stood up and forced his way through the pirates to snarl at the prisoner whilst another pirate kicked him.

"He's a strong lad; he should guard the treasure well." Marcus shouted to William as the pirates dispersed to continue with their activities, ahead of clapping and shouting, thoroughly whilst enjoying dancing from the dancers. The dancing stopped abruptly when a pirate grabbed a boy that had been clearing glasses from tables.

"Top me up now!" He ordered banging his cup fiercely on the table, before he tore of the patch that covered his damaged eye. This startled the young boy as Marcus continued banging his glass frantically on the table intimidating the boy further, who nervously picked up the glass then dropped it.

This angered William he towered over the timid boy that coward on the floor.

"I will deal with you later," He shouted at whilst continuing his card game.

The boy quickly stood up when noticing the prisoner that was also on the floor.

All the pirates laughed and jeered while William turned to the prisoner.

"What's your name boy?" He asked.

The prisoner was petrified of William's mean, grimacing smile.

"Jo." He replied nervously.

William gave him an evil stare before looking over at Marcus.

"Feed him well! He's got a very important job ahead of him." William said.

The pirates had gathered on the highest hill of the island they had dug a deep hole and was throwing sacks of gold and fine jewellery into it.

The pirates dragged Jo towards the hole and then suddenly there was a loud bang as a deep wound emerged on his back, causing him to fall . . . Another shot caused him to wriggle in agony. He lay still on the floor as the mean evil William walked towards him holding the piston he had used to kill him. He then kicked him into the hole with the treasure.

"Guard my gold well!" He jeered then turned and walked away leaving the other pirates to fill in the hole.

CHAPTER 9

Jo

It was May 1924 when the rumours that William Thomas's hoard of treasure had been discovered in a small town in Palmer's on the site with deep excavation work to construct the new school.

Jack Mimes and his brother Fred were young delinquents that had over heard the shopkeeper and a customer discussing it. They listen keenly to the news that spread throughout Latin Town.

Jack was the older of the brother's who was a notorious villain that often robbed shops, houses and terrorized the town. Jack had often escaped the wrath of the law. He had decided to make Fred his accomplice now that he had come of age.

Both brothers hastily left the shop discussing all the possibilities that would lead them to the hoard of treasure then finally agreeing a plan to retrieve it.

"We'll get the Sergeant if there's ever such a hoard of treasure he'll be the man to take us to it." Jack said as the two brothers became convinced that Sergeant Wilson was their man.

Their target still dressed in a green uniform was about to finish his shift. He sat snoring at his desk when there was a disturbance, which made him rush to his feet checking each cell before switching the lights out and leaving the constabulary; at this time the two brothers ambushed him.

They took him deep in the valleys and marshes of Stone Harbour where they persistently beat and kicked him, as they forced him to tell them where the hoard of treasure was.

"Take us to it!" Jack ordered as the seagent lay tied up and defenceless on the ground.

"I don't know anything, it's all a big mistake." Sergeant Wilson, cried.

By now the brothers continued to attack him because he unaware of the treasure's location as he screamed in agony.

"I've heard it's been deposited in the marshes near here, for safe keeping!" He yelled. Then the beating stopped and the brothers dragged him high into the marshes, where he pointed to a spot that was very unfamiliar to him. He thought it strange that he had chosen to stop there.

Suddenly Jack pulled out his gun and fired a shot at him that caused him to wriggle before he collapsed.

The sweat poured off the brothers backs from the digging which was leaving them extremely frustrated when they were unable to retrieve the treasure.

"Where is it?" Fred asked ahead of resting on the handle of his shovel.

"Keep digging" Jack ordered.

They continued to dig deeper, but still they could not retrieve the treasure; just as they were about to rest they hit on something that caused them to stop and then they proceeded hurling it out quickly to discover the remains of a skeleton.

There was a loud noise followed by flashes of light accompanied by Jo still covered with bruising on his face and the gunshot wounds were still visible on his clothing.

The brothers became terrified as they trembled then scarpered.

Sergeant Wilson wriggled into the bushes fearing the brothers would return to kill him; he was completely unaware about why they had left in that fashion.

Charlie was resting on a hill close to the harbour when he saw the two brothers running towards the sea, this he thought strange and then he began to hear strange noises.

On investigating he walked towards tall bushes where he discovered the injured Sergeant badly beaten; he pulled the Sergeant from the bushes.

"Thank you." Sergeant Wilson said whilst trying to stand up, but fell back down.

Charlie immediately noticed the blood gashing from his arm.

"You've been shot! We need to tend to that wound." Charlie insisted.

There was boiling water in a small tin on a fire beside the fire was the bullet that he removed from the Sergeant's arm; there was blood stained clothing which Charlie used to clean and dress the wound before elevating it in a sling.

Charlie had prepared fresh fish for the Sergeant, who stretched awkwardly to receive it.

"It tastes really good." He said as he bit into it savagely.

Charlie smiled with contentment at the gratitude the Sergeant had shown towards him as he began to explain what he had encountered:

"I was just finishing my shift. I was coming through the gates of the constabulary when two men, continually beat me because they wanted the hoard of treasure that belonged to William Thomas the famous pirate.

Then the strangest thing happened a sailor appeared from nowhere I thought I had fallen asleep. Then I realised I was not sleeping and there was no sign of the sailor.

I think it was the sailor who guards the treasure that led me to that particular spot and then he led you to me; he who guard's the treasure." He said almost as if he was telling a story.

Charlie was not impressed by what the Sergeant said. What nonsense he thought.

"You have had a very bad ordeal and you have suffered an injury to your head it's time to rest now" Charlie ordered.

Sergeant Wilson had a lot more to say to him and was not ready to shut up just yet.

"They shot me because they knew I would recognize them, one face was familiar, but I cannot recall it," The, Sergeant continued.

Charlie felt sorry for the Sergeant he was very helpless and clearly the ordeal had affected him.

"I'm sorry nobody deserves that." He said whilst pitying the Sergeant.

"It's, Sergeant Wilson of the Jamaican constabulary." He said stretching his hand to Charlie who shook it and at the same time introduced himself: "Charlie."

They both relaxed by the fire prior to Charlie noticing the fire dying down and immediately stacked it with more wood.

"How did you come to be here?" Sergeant Wilson asked.

"I don't know. I remember waiting for a train that would take me to Earth." He replied tending the fire before he continued with the conversation.

"What year is this?" He asked looking at the Sergeant strangely.

"You're confused, why 25, January 1924." The, Sergeant replied.

Charlie remembered the clock spinning around fast prior to realizing he had returned to Earth, but was in a different age.

"Where is this place?" He asked.

"Why Palmer's Stone Harbour." The Sergeant answered as he continued to look at Charlie in a trance like state of mind:

"This was where the pirates would bring their ships, why just over there you would have about four or five pirate ships all anchored, waiting to be repaired. They often came ashore to fill their hungry bellies and to sell the hijacked merchant ships often filled with treasure. They were very evil pirates that came to bury the treasure."

Charlie listened keenly whilst the Sergeant continued the story.

"William Thomas was the most notorious pirate of the Caribbean Sea. He was one of the most famous sea robbers of all time. At first he was a sailor then he went to Port Royal where he acquired leadership of a ship called the Purple Pearl. He did outstanding work for the British Crown and received attention from generals, common sailors, soldiers and the respect of all captains in the Caribbean Sea thanks to his skills, cleverness and brightness. It was his flagship, where he spent his free time and from where he operated all of his robber's actions, legal sea fight and even wild inordinate drunken activities. The story as it his flagship has been seen sailing the seas of the Caribbean; it was right here this very shore; this very place where he often anchored, rested with his crew and repaired ships damaged in fights. The coral cliffs are said to house millions of treasures belonging to The Purple Pearl."

The fire began to die down thus Charlie piled on more wood.

"Wow! That was some story." Charlie was clearly impressed by what the Sergeant had told him . . .

"Look, Look!" The Sergeant shouted frantically as he pointed far out to sea. Charlie followed his finger which led to a pirate flag that blew freely before vanishing into the horizon.

"Did you see that?" Sergeant Wilson asked.

Charlie had seen what appeared to be a pirate flag, but he shook his head he was not about to be agreeing to something so extraordinary.

Sergeant Wilson was fast asleep beside the fire whilst Charlie watched the fire, becoming mesmerized by thoughts of him lost in a time he knew nothing about when a bright light suddenly appeared causing him to shield away.

Stepping out of the light was a young man dressed in sailor's clothes. Charlie shocked by the figure covered in bruises, whip marks and gunshot wounds. He looked at Charlie, with blood still fresh on his face.

"I am, Jo the guardian of William Thomas's Treasure. You have shown great kindness by helping a dying man. You used your skills to save him and you caught fish and fed him. I will make you the beneficiary of the treasure that I am guarding." He said.

The white sand rumbled over unearthing sacks of jewellery and sacks of gold coins. Charlie looked in disbelief.

"This is yours to unearth whenever you choose." Jo said.

The treasure sank deep back into the ground whilst Charlie watched then, Jo noticed; Charlie's clothes and sensed a spiritual presence opposed to a physical one prior realizing Charlie was from a different time.

"You are a lost soul here; you do not belong in this time zone." He inquisitively stressed.

Charlie agreed by nodding his head."

"I can take you back to where you have come from, but you will have to fulfil your mission," He said holding Charlie's hand and then disappearing with him.

Linda continued to bang on the window of the ticket hall, but Charlie remained stretched out on the floor. The clock began to tick loudly and then she witnessed a small movement from his fingers.

"Charlie, Charlie!" She shouted frantically.

Charlie stumbled to his feet and Jo was still standing beside him he could hear Linda calling him as he walked towards her with Jo. Jo opened the window to let Charlie climb through whilst the clock spun forwards.

"Thank you, thank you," Charlie said showing immense gratitude to Jo for bringing him back.

Jo smiled at him as he focused on the clock spinning faster forward; it chimed six times then Jo vanished.

Charlie was aware that the communication room had links with many different worlds, but you were never sure of finding the right one. Charlie looked at Linda, who had a compelled look on her face.

"Charlie, who were you talking to just then?" She asked.

"Somebody, that helped me back." He replied.

"You didn't go anywhere and I didn't see anyone with you." She questioned.

"Time is hidden in a clock" He replied.

CHAPTER 10

Transposing Carriages

Linda and Charlie paced up and down the waiting room constantly checking the destination board, but the train had not arrived. Unexpectedly the board flashed and the destinations returned informing them that the next train would be departing from "Nowhere" in approximately fifth teen minutes. On entering the platform they noticed red crystal balls peering at them through the mist, puzzled to what it was; something suddenly rushed into the waiting room; it was a black cat.

"Where did that cat come from?" Scott asked.

Everyone watched the cat as he jumped onto the bench which activated the screen again where Emily became visable inside a church with high ceilings, large, arched, stained windows were all around her along with murals of biblical heroes. This was where she often prayed for her mother and brothers safe return.

The sun shone brightly that day which left her believing in her prayers as she walked along the busy high road then turned into a side road towards her home, when appearing before her was a black cat that lay injured and panting on the curb, she quickly took off her coat and wrapped it around the injured black cat ahead of rushing to the vet.

On arrival at the veterinary surgery the door closed immediately after the vet had taken the cat, leaving Emily waiting patiently until the vet returned to question her.

"What happened?" He asked.

Emily explained how she had found the cat whilst walking home:

"I was walking home and noticed him hurt and injured lying in the road, so I rushed him here".

"He's not your cat then?" The vet asked.

"No!" She replied.

"He was very Lucky to find you. I'll do all I can for Luck" the vet said absorbing Emily's reaction to the vet calling the cat Luck. Emily smiled approvingly ahead of waiting impatiently for news about him.

Meanwhile back at the waiting room Luck remained seated on the bench as they all stood huddled around the screen listening keenly to what the vet had to say when he returned:

"Well I've treated his wounds the best I can he's seemed to have fallen into a deep sleep, but we will monitor his progress." He said handing Emily his card.

"You can call whenever you want to find out how he's doing." He continued.

Linda, Charlie and Scott made there way to the platform. Fog light were seen in the mist that got brighter as the most beautiful train pulled into the platform with white carriages which had golden and platinum murals of wild animals; some displayed golden horses others had cows and lambs set around the stars and the moon. There were eight shinning carriages aligned on the platform. There were golden handles attached to the doors that suddenly flung open to reveal golden steps. They all stood gob smacked bewildered by the beauty when Linda remembered that Luck and Charlie were the unfamiliar names on the tickets she had retrieved from the hatch.

She rushed into the waiting room grabbing the cat then raced back onto the platform. Prior to them all entering the carriage via the golden steps.

On entering the carriage they were stunned by the young children, teenagers and adults inside that waved frantically at them when they walked through admiring the passenger's costumes which appeared to be from all eras and different parts of the world. Their eyes focused on the Egyptians and Romans from centuries gone by that sat silently on the seats.

There were children dressed in Victorian clothes playing when Linda opened a cubicle door. She gasped then suddenly the children stopped playing as the train transformed from a beautiful carriage to a misty street in London with rats running out of piles of discarded rubbish. The children held hands as they formed a circle singing nursery rhymes outside houses, which had red crosses painted above the doors. When Linda approached none of them noticed her she waved frantically for their response, but they could not see her. She then noticed a nurse knocking on a door with a red cross above it, she walked over to her:

"Hello" she said but the nurse did not notice her either the door slowly opened.

"Rosy" The nurse said as the women dressed in an apron with hair neatly pulled back nodded on opening the door fully.

"Hello Marie." She said solemnly before leading her through the house.

Linda followed Marie the district nurse and a frequent visitor to the house.

Rosie's s face was red from crying and she looked timid and withdrawn when leading Marie to a large room, where three children laid on beds with large blotches on their faces. Marie approached the first child and gave him a spoon of medicine and then she moved on to the second child, but noticed he did not wake up. She watched Rosy burst into tears when covering over the young child with a blanket.

"I'm really sorry." She said dropping her head to the floor her sympathy was with Rosy who had lost a child; she sat her down and then tended the third child handing her liquorices and medicine.

"I'll be back in a week she said leaving Rosy distraught and beside herself.

Linda followed her out the house to see large rats jumping out at the children that had been carrying small flowers. Rosie squirmed on sighting them and then noticed the two horses with carriages filled with families and their possessions leaving the city. She watched quietly until a man with a large top hat emerged from another carriage filled with cats and dogs. He had a large net which he used to sneak up to a stray dog before capturing him; he then noticed Marie coming out of the house "Hello, Marie." He shouted to her.

Marie was very distressed about the loss of her patient she was slow to acknowledged her friend Sid. "Hello Sid." She shouted.

"I have caught a few more for the slaughter." He said putting the captured dog into the cage. Marie became more distressed when she saw how many cats and dogs Sid had captured.

"Are they all going to be slaughtered?" She asked him.

"Yes, these are the causes of the terrible disease" He told her. She was very upset to see so many animals slaughtered and then she remembered her patient.

"I lost another patient today." She told him.

Sid sympathised with her knowing that her job was stressful especially when she lost her patients.

"I will be leaving for the country tomorrow." He said.

Marie often dreamt about escaping to the country and was chuffed that Sid had managed to leave.

"It's the safest place right now; you will be safer there." She said.

"You be careful Miss. You know you could come down at any time." He warned.

"I have my flowers." she said as she produced a pocket of red roses. Sid smiled then drove away.

Marie was about to walk away when she saw another horse and cart pulling up with a man dressed in black. He looked at Marie as she pointed to the house she had just left.

"Bring out your dead!" The man shouted knocking on Rosie's door.

Linda solemnly walked away before becoming aware of thick heavy smoke choking her; she then noticed the children had stopped singing and was coughing uncontrollably whilst fire trucks rushed over to burning buildings in the distance.

The people ran out of the smoke filled area whilst the children continued to sing:

"London Bridge is burning down, burning down my fair lady." Linda then became aware of the fire spreading throughout the city which was causing people to flee their homes. She tried to escape the fire by running down the cobblestone pavement when she got further away the singing got louder.

"A ring a ring of roses, a pocketful of posies: Atischoo, atischoo we all fall down."

Linda looked back at the burning city that miraculously transformed back to the carriage, where the singing continued as the children played and joked in the beautiful carriages.

Linda closed the cubicle door "I'm so thankful I wasn't living in those times."

Charlie and Linda peeped through the windows of more cubicles noticing that most of them were full of wounded soldiers from wars gone by and young children travelling alone. Linda opened a cubicle door inside was a young girl wearing a scarf and clutching a brown leather bag "Are there any spare seats in here?" She asked.

"No. I am sorry miss." The girl replied.

Linda was about to shut the door when the girl asked "Have you seen my brother miss?"

"No sorry I haven't" Linda answered. Again she was about to shut the door, but the girl spoke.

"Lukas got separated. I know he's on this train!"

Linda smiled at the worried girl who appeared desperate to find her brother.

"If I see him I will let him know you are looking for him." She said.

"Jana My name is Jana." She said then stretched her hand which Linda shook whilst she introduced herself. "Linda" She smiled then closed the cubicle door and then turned to Charlie: "There are so many soldiers and so many children here!" She said.

Charlie peeped through the cubicle window saddened by so many young people.

"These are the victims of war!" He replied as his hand became stuck on the cubicle handle that suddenly vibrated, shaking the whole carriage, causing them all to stumble to the floor. Prior to them noticing the marble floor had turned to dust. Again the cubicle transformed into a city reduced to rumble. Linda stood face to face with the soldiers that paroled the city, but they could not see her. The soldiers checked the burnt out buildings for civilians caught up in the crossfire; on entering the building there were numerous women and children killed in the bloodbath.

Laid out on the stretcher was a young woman dressed in a scarf beside her was a brown leather bag. Linda immediately recognized her it was Jana the girl she had met in the cubicles. She stared at her lifeless body before the building reverted back to its original state leaving Linda feeling as if she was about to watch a movie:

It was a bright sunny morning and the family was about to have breakfast when Jana's father broke the devastating news.

Her father Mute was part of the army he received the letter stating, Lukas and Jana would be joining the youth movements and they would be leaving tomorrow. Jana's mother, Isabella was devastated.

"They are only children. I won't let them go." Isabella cried.

"You're going to stop them?" Mute argued.

"Yes, they'll be killed" Isabella said.

"We cannot go against high officials, they must go!" Mute shouted.

"For years they convened the restrictions of the underage youth, why now millions of children are wearing the army uniform, Lukas digging tank traps and manning aircraft-batteries; now they're saying that Lukas will go into combat. We are their parents! We must protect them!"

Isabella yelled.

"We will be killed; we have got to obey the ruling of the high officials!

This is government procedure the younger generation must be mobilized; you want to go against that? You know about the new policy all able bodied people are required to serve"

Mute continued.

Isabella wept she was powerless. She could not stop her children joining the youth movement.

Two weeks later Isabella received the telegram stating Jana and Lukas was missing. She was devastated she broke down and cried uncontrollably.

"My babies they have taken away my babies!" She wept.

Mute tried to control her, but it was hopeless she raged frantically throwing the cutlery at him as he ran through the door trying to escape injury.

CHAPTER 11

Jason

Linda felt very sad for Isabella when she woke up to find herself back on the white marble floor shouting for Charlie and Scott to get up. They all continued through the carriages arriving at a cubicle which displayed their names illuminated in white lettering above the door. Scott was the first to notice and shouted "This is our cubicle."

He opened the door and inside a soldier lay snoring across the seats with a green army sack beside him.

Charlie and Linda followed Scott inside the cubicle.

"Hello, you're in our cubicle!" Linda said.

The soldier awoke giving Linda a loving smile. Linda smiled back nervously and they all made themselves comfortable on the seats.

"Jason." The soldier said as he held out his hand for Linda, she shook his hand and in turn the soldier shook Charlie and Scott's hand respectively; he looked at Linda and then noticed Luck popping his head out of her bag.

"Who may this be?" He asked.

Luck licked Linda's hand continuously before Jason stretched his hand for Luck to lick.

Linda remembered how Emily found the cat and then how the cat found them and then she recalled the vet naming him.

"Luck!" She said.

Jason continued to stroke Luck.

They were all sitting comfortably on their seats waiting for the train to depart when thick steam smothered the carriage window which Jason wiped away with his hands as the train speeded out of the platform.

Peeping through the window he witnessed the train speeding through mountains, valleys and high over clouds showing scenes set in beautiful green pastures and sandy beaches.

He cleaned the window but the thick mist appeared again then mysteriously a portrait of all four of them appeared on the window.

He tried to alert the others, but the portrait vanished leaving them less than impressed by his story. He looked towards the window again and the portraits returned.

"Look!" He shouted.

The portrait quickly vanished leaving them all staring at a misty window. Linda stroked Lucks head before concluding that tiredness was the reasons for his sudden outburst when Jason began pointing and shouted for their attention once more and they all focused on the window.

The firing jets flew over the battlefield depositing bombs, whilst soldiers ran for cover.

Dead and injured soldiers were a prominent sight beneath the smoke, rubble and destruction of the smoke filled battlefield. An injured soldier huddled on a large rock beneath the grey skies which suddenly cracked displaying white lights throughout. The skies roared loudly and then heavy rain poured down on the soldier with his army sack strapped to his back he screamed then clutched an injured knee whilst the rain-washed away the thick red blood that ran along the rock. He tore his shirt and attempted to bandage his knee, but found he was too weak; he slumped across the rock closing his eyes and waited for the end.

When all hope seemed lost running through the explosives and burning fires someone was calling him:

"Jason, Jason." Was heard throughout the battlefield ahead of the window steaming up; they all looked at Jason now fully aware he was the injured soldier.

"That's you!" Charlie shouted as Jason nodded and then cleaned the window.

The voice became clearer as he approached Jason still slumbered on the rock.

"Here, here!" Jason shouted.

He did not shout in vain another soldier became visible through the fires, the bombs and the heavy rain. The soldier ran towards him carrying a rucksack he kneeled beside him and removed items from a box.

"Jason, Jason." He said.

He was worried about the amount of blood lost when he dressed his injured knee.

"You will make it Jason; you just need to hold on" The soldier told him.

Jason did not respond as the soldier carried him through the burning fires dodging missiles and landmines; there were burning fires and explosives all around them which were choking them.

Finally they arrived at the land rover Jason was laid down inside before the soldier slammed the door and drove out of the battlefields dodging the gunshots and missiles.

Once out of the danger zone the soldier went to check on Jason he rocked him, but he did not utter a word and his eyes remained closed. It became apparent to the soldier that if Jason did not get the right medical attention he would die; he turned to leave him when Jason whispered to him:

"I'm not going to make it Jimmy!"

Jimmy rubbed his shoulder to comfort him.

"We are all goners." He said realising he had chosen the wrong words; he continued to try harder to encourage him to hold on to his life.

"You're a fighter; you will come through Jason!" He said.

All eyes were fixed on the steamed window and then Jason looked at Charlie with real worry in his eyes. Charlie looked away from him.

"I'll pull through mate I'm a fighter." He said.

The train continued its journey with them all peering through the window that occasionally filled with mist. A large green and blue ball was visible set in the darkness of the universe.

"Look, its Earth," Scott shouted as every one peered out the window to see planet Earth that appeared like a large football they continued to stare captured in their thoughts of their lives they were desperate to return too. The Earth got smaller as the train sped further away from it. They all remained slouched in their seats captivated by their own thoughts when a great force opened the cubicle door along with a loud voice addressing them.

"Can I see your tickets please?" The voice said leaving them bamboozled to where the voice was coming from because no one appeared to be there, until Charlie pointed to the tiny figure, no bigger than a pin head standing at the foot of the door stretching his hand for the tickets and getting larger by the second. He transformed to a tall, well-built ticket inspector with a stern, threatening face that demanded the tickets again.

"Can I see your tickets please?" He repeated.

"We don't have any tickets!" Charlie replied looking directly at the inspector whom stared back angrily.

"You will have to get off the train!" He announced while he walking towards the window still focusing on Charlie who had shrunk to the size of a mouse; he picked him up and threw him out the window.

"Stop, stop!" Linda screamed. As they rushed over to the window, but all they could see was a spec disappearing into the darkness; they remained silent and stunned by what they witnessed. Everyone looked at the Ticket Inspector horrified by his actions and then out of the window in disbelief that Charlie was gone. The silence was broken when Linda turned to the Inspector in disgust:

"What have you done?" She asked.

"You need a valid ticket to enter this train!" He said.

"Bring him back immediately!" Jason ordered.

The Ticket Inspector then focused on Jason as he suddenly began to get smaller. He struggled to stop the Inspector throwing him out of the window.

Linda and Scott went over to the window Jason too became a spec that vanished into the darkness leaving Linda devastated about her friends, when she suddenly remembered the tickets she had retrieved from the waiting room. The Ticket Inspector was setting his sights on Scott who was using his hands to shield away from the Inspector's glare, but he too began to diminish.

"Stop, Stop!" She screamed, but the Ticket Inspector continued to focus on Scott. Linda opened her bag and Luck ran out this seemed to break the Inspector's concentration and Scott immediately regained his normal size. Then Linda screamed: "I have the tickets!" She shouted while producing all the ticket's she collected from the machine which she handed to him. He scrutinized each ticket in turn and then said:" You had the tickets, all this time!"

Linda felt ashamed of herself for totally forgetting about the tickets as well as blaming herself for the ruthless treatment Charlie and Jason encountered.

"I didn't know you wanted those tickets." She whispered quietly.

The Ticket Inspector clipped each ticket in turn and gave the tickets back to her which she put back into her bag, ahead of noticing two beautiful pairs of golden feathered wings that appeared on each shoulder blade of Scott which was causing him to wiggle off his seat.

"Sit still!" Linda ordered.

"Wow!" Scott shouted on noticing Linda's wings.

The Ticket Inspector stopped writing in his book then smiled approvingly. Linda refused to smile back as she was very angry with him because her thoughts were with her friends.

"What about our friends?" She asked; he was unsympathetic towards her as she waited calmly for a response from him.

"They have arrived on another planet; they must try and board the train; they too will acquire wings that may help them or they may be captured by the inhabitants; I will let the train operators know I have seen the tickets; if you're Lucky you may meet them at the next station." He said showing no remorse for his actions which left Linda very worried about her friends, but she dare not voice her anger in case he decided to throw her out of the window too.

Scott continued to examine his mother's golden wings which were soft with millions of fluffy golden feathers attached to small, golden, stalks that fitted smug on her shoulder blade.

The Ticket Inspector smiled when he saw how happy Scott was after receiving his wings.

"They will take a bit of getting use to, they do vanish without warning, but don't worry because they will reappear; good bye!"

He slammed the door then transformed back into a small person that walked briskly to the next cubicle.

Linda was still very annoyed with him.

"Arrogant and evil that Ticket Inspector; what's happened to Charlie and Jason I do hope they are safe." She said.

Scott became worried about his friends too they both cuddled as Linda reassured him that they would see their friends again.

Linda and Scott were getting use to their wings and could not wait to try them out. Scott tested them around the cubicle he managed to fly up to the ceiling with them, but soon came crashing back down this startled, Luck who jumped back into Linda's bag.

"There is clearly not enough space in this cubicle for you to test those wings!" Linda told him; she was amused when she gasped Scott laying flat out on the floor without his wings.

Scott was disappointed about losing his wings because he was very fond of them.

"What happened to my wings mum?" He asked whilst feeling his back desperate for his wings to reappear. Linda noticed his anguish and cuddled him this made Scott aware that her wings had also disappeared; he remembered what the Ticket Inspector told him about the wings disappearing and settled back down. They both sat quietly their thoughts were with their friends.

CHAPTER 12

The Aliens

Charlie and Jason came crashing down onto the ground covered in green, slimy, grime which they tried to clean. They were very tired and sweaty from the sun's rays that beamed down on them through the blue and red clouds that hovered above. They moved away and used the plants with huge, purple, stalks and yellow mushroom heads to shield themselves. It then became impossible for them to breathe as they both tried to stand, but collapse coughing and choking whilst blocking their eyes from the brightness. Beneath the mushrooms whispering and talking could be heard whilst they both continued to shield their faces from the light. They then made several more attempts to lift themselves to their feet, but collapsed again.

Mimi and Kiwi hid behind the bushes as their shadow emerged on the sandy ground beneath the hovering blue and red clouds.

A prominent square box was affiliated to their chest. Kiwi tampers with the buttons and colourful wires that appeared inside the opened box.

"They need oxygen to survive. We will need to give them the microbe that produces oxygen." Kiwi said before hunting for a plant that was dispatched on the ground which he picked before feeding it to Charlie and Jason. Moments after they opened their eyes fully and were able to stand up.

Kiwi hid behind the bushes and operated buttons from his box which generated beams directly at Charlie, and Jason which immediately dysfunction them.

Kiwi and Mimi looked on at Charlie and Jason, with large wide eyes that protruded their huge round heads. Their bodies were slim with very long arms with slit hands.

They looked identical, but there were differences in their appearance when they emerged from the bushes. Kiwi had large blue eyes while Mimi had small red ones and Kiwi was slightly taller.

They stared in disbelief at the two humans parading around like zombies in circles.

The skies became red when the blue clouds disappeared leaving the climate very warm.

"We must notify father immediately!" Kiwi said.

"No, no they look harmless father will put them in captivity and carryout experiments on them." Mimi said which made them argue continuously about what action to take. There was a sense of brotherly rivalry between them. Mimi appeared to be a humble peacemaker whilst Kiwi appeared to despise his brother because he was more intelligent and considerate than him.

They walked towards Charlie and Jason. Kiwi's box displayed scans of Jason and Charlie's whole body; drawings appeared displaying results of the inner thigh, head circumference and other mathematical results before displaying the planet Earth and the result which read. "Human, Planet Earth." This excited Kiwi.

"I knew it.!" He said.

He immediately beamed a high voltage at Jason and Charlie which caused them to vanish. Mimi became angry at his brothers action.

"Why did you do that?" Mimi shouted as Kiwi gave him a long, hard stare.

"All the time, I have had to sit back and listen to father praise you. Father prefers you he has taught you everything. This is my one chance to please father and I won't let you ruin it." Kiwi replied then paused for a short while before continuing.

"Father must know I'm the better son. He must know that I captured the human's it was my discovery. I am guaranteed now to be the true ruler and you my brother will be just my servant." Kiwi continued.

He beamed the beam again before disappearing himself leaving Mimi alone and disillusioned.

Mimi acted quickly he opened the box and pressed rewind and immediately Kiwi, Jason and Charlie returned and then before Kiwi could act Mimi pressed another button and then Kiwi vanished.

"No more botheration from my stupid brother" He said.

Mimi watched as Jason and Charlie slowly recovered from the zombie state Kiwi left them in and soon regained consciousness. Mimi knew they were harmless and gestured at them to follow him.

"Come quick!" Mimi shouted then vanished inside the bushes.

Charlie had injured his back and foot which made it difficult for him to walk. Jason helped to support him as they followed Mimi into the bushes.

Coming out of the bushes they noticed many spaceships deposited all around in the open fields. Mimi stepped out into the fields with Charlie and Jason who stood helpless behind him.

He stroked their hair before feeling their faces then stared at them in disbelief as he examined their arms and legs which appeared odd because he had never been this close to humans.

Charlie and Jason looked at him the alien whose head and body was almost transparent and with his brain clearly visible.

Mimi gestured again for them to follow him as they ran across towards a large spaceship with Mimi assisting Charlie who was struggling to keep up.

They found themselves hurrying through the green and yellow fields with huge illuminated, colourful weeds, bushes and plants and many different size spaceships situated all around them that hovered above the ground.

Mimi led them through more plants and trees there were larger flying saucers deposited all around them. Then he stood at a spaceship to operate a little button from his box and the flying saucer opened allowing them all to enter via a huge staircase that emerged.

Inside the spaceship there were wires and buttons that were clearly visible through the large screens and computer workstations around the spacious dwellings; there were many round platforms made from stone with blue beams attached underneath them.

"You are good humans?" Mimi asked.

Jason and Charlie nodded.

"Planet Earth is visible to us we often send space ships there. You are solid beings and we are transparent we are from electrical energy your source is a different energy." Mimi said.

He stopped talking when he noticed Charlie was in a lot of discomfort he stretched out his arm and massaged Charlie's shoulder relieving him from all his pain. Charlie was extremely grateful to him.

The alien introduced himself to Charlie and Jason and they introduced themselves to him.

"Mimi."

"Charlie."

"Jason,"

Mimi explained that they were in great danger from the ruler who was his father and the seniors.

"If you are discovered they will be put you in captivity and you will be experimented on."

He said, before the spaceship slowly began to open which caused Mimi to rush over to the workstation where he operate a few buttons that prevented the opening of the spaceship.

Outside the spaceship many residents gathered all the aliens armed with electronic lasers which fired high voltage electrical beams. They shot at the spaceship and protested outside. Mustafa was Kiwi and Mimi's father who was the most senior alien that governed the planet his fellow aliens shouted and threatened him: "Your son is harbouring human's that is a very serious offence Mustafa we will deal with him if we catch him." The alien warned.

"If Mimi is guilty of such an offence he will be dealt with appropriately."

Mustafa said whilst he shrugged free from the angry aliens, before challenging the alien that was the main instigator of the problems.

"I'm the highest senior here how dare you question my authority. If he is guilty I will punish him . . . We must investigate these allegations now." Mustafa said.

Meanwhile, Mimi sat at the workstation watching everything that was happening outside. He became very worried before explaining to Charlie and Jason what was happening.

"You must wait here I will try to protect you, but my evil brother has notified father and the seniors they are here." He said.

Charlie and Jason were grateful to Mimi, but they became very worried about what the aliens would do if they captured them. Mimi looked worried he knew that the spaceship was no longer safe.

"I will try to take you to the station you may be able to continue your journey." You have wings now!" He said looking down at Charlie's wing.

"What wings?" Charlie questioned.

Charlie and Jason were shocked when they saw the golden wings attached to their shoulder blades, but they could only examine them for a short while before the wings vanished.

The seniors managed to enter the spaceship with Kiwi at the forefront he was the one that led Mustafa and all the senior aliens to the spaceship. Mustafa stepped forward.

"Mimi I am very disappointed with you! Why would you put shame on your family this way?" He said.

Mimi was sad that his father was angry with him because he shared a strong bond with him and always strived to make him proud.

"Father, I only tried to help them." Mimi, said.

"You know our policy on humans." Mustafa shouted while Kiwi stepped forward.

"Father, he had no intention of informing you; he tried to lure me into to his plans, but I refused to betray you and our planet!" Kiwi insisted whilst the aliens cheered Kiwi who was very popular with the other aliens.

"It's all lies; it's a web of lies." Mimi shouted.

"Father, it's the truth I tell you! Mimi is trying to help them escape; he cannot be trusted and he has betrayed us!" Kiwi shouted with the angry aliens standing beside him, with age lines protruding through their foreheads, that signified age and seniority accompanied with evil. Mimi was fearful of the angry aliens before him.

They were shocked and angry, to see Charlie and Jason and then turned to Mimi.

"Punish him; take him to the prison, hypocrite, traitor," were just some of the names that Mimi was called whilst continuing to defend himself.

"These are humans from planet Earth that I found in the fields."

The alien figures became angrier, one-stepped forward before shouting at Mimi.

"Oh, what have you done? Why did you bring them here?" The alien said as he pressed buttons situated on his chest that caused the whole spaceship to go dark and suddenly a light beamed on Jason and Charlie as they vanished from where they stood into the round pedestal surrounded by green light; every time they tried to move off the pedestals they were electrically shocked.

Mustafa then ordered the aliens to capture Mimi:" Take Him!"

"Father, Father!" Mimi shouted.

"You have betrayed us, you will be punished!" Mustafa said.

All the aliens began walking towards Mimi, whom tried to escape by running through to the stairway that exited the saucer, but they beamed their lasers and he fell helpless before they captured him and dragged him away.

Many aliens gathered in a large flying saucer where they all sat neatly in rows of benches which formed a semi-circle. On the centre stage were two spotlights which beamed down from the ceiling; every alien sat in silence all focused on the beam which changed from a white to grey before changing to a dull beam then suddenly trapped in the beam of light was Jason and Charlie. All the aliens gasped at the humans trapped in the beam of light.

Shore was a lead scientist on Earth projects he emerged patrolling around Jason and Charlie and then addressed the shocked audience.

"We have earthlings amongst us; many times we have sent missions to Earth in the forms of flying saucers which were capable of flying hundred's of light years in just twenty four hours. We could only land for a short time because we were not immune to the climate change." Shore said then he raised his voice at the audience who listened keenly.

"We even deposited our very own pets on Earth unfamiliar with the climate the frogs adapted to Earth life very well as they adjusted to the balance of oxygen and water." Shore continued.

The audience all choked with laughter at Shore's words before Shore raised his voice higher.

"Enough! Enough of the frogs. I am giving you earthlings. Today I am giving you the humans themselves." shore announced.

Shore pointed to Charlie and Jason then invited the audience to come and examine them the aliens emerged from each row consecutively when they reached the pedestals they gathered around Charlie and Jason and sliced the beam with their hands then prodded and poked them. Which made their skin turn blue because they were pinched so many times.

Charlie and Jason turned on the pedestal when all the aliens left. Unable to move they were both desperate to communicate with each other, but even to speak signified movement and they were electrically shocked.

"Charlie." Jason called at the same time he was electrically shocked and left screeching in agony.

Charlie groaned to acknowledge him which made the pain less severe.

"Mm" he responded as Jason prepared himself for the agonizing pain he was about to encounter because he continued to speak. "How will we get out of here?" He asked.

Charlie could only shake his head in response.

Far away from the alien city was the prison, which was a large flying saucer hovering above the ground. Inside rows of pedestals housed alien incapacitated by strong beams of light spinning around on a pedestal was Mimi he was injured and weak from the laser the seniors used to capture him and the beams of light that kept shocking him every time he moved; this caused his head to droop towards the ground with his eyes closed.

Mustafa came to see him he was very sad because Mimi had caused a lot of embarrassment to his family and he had jeopardized his position. Mustafa was also heartbroken that his favourite son was now a prisoner.

"I'm sorry father, but I did not have the heart to destroy the humans or to see them destroyed, because they are different. If I'm to be punished for not being evil I stand by my beliefs." Mimi said.

"These humans are dangerous!" Mustafa said.

"I scanned for danger and it came back harmless they're not dangerous father!" He said.

"Why did you betray me son? You know the rules pertaining to foreign invaders. You know that all I have and have achieved was for you and your brother; your mother is devastated how do I get you out of this situation without losing my title, my home and my respect." Mustafa cried.

"Father let me rescue my friends, we will think of something, they will destroy them and Shore will try to make as much money from them so he can get your title; we must let them go! Shore can take the blame we must stop him." Mimi pleaded.

Mustafa immediately ordered his son's release ahead of Mimi heading straight to the flying saucer where Charlie and Jason were captive.

Charlie and Jason remained on the pedestals held by the light beam that continued to inflict pain on both of them as they continued to communicate with each other.

Mimi emerged rushing towards the workstation, which he disarmed releasing Charlie and Jason. They were happy to see Mimi alive and well. Charlie and Jason jumped off the beams stretching their arms and legs completely unaware of the formation of their wings. Mimi looked at them with terror on his face, he was aware of the danger that befalls each of them.

"They are planning a congress tomorrow. We will take our chances then" He announced as Charlie and Jason flew around the flying saucer with their golden wings. Then a flashing red light appeared on the work station, it was detecting the presents of the Journey Train

"You can fly out of here now the train is near, use your wings and try to board the train again!" Mimi instructed.

Charlie and Jason acknowledged Mimi and flew towards the exit of the flying saucer then waited for Mimi to release the doors. Suddenly Mimi heard alien voices which made him order Jason and Charlie to get back on the pedestals and immediately switched the beams back before hiding behind a large white pillar.

They stood silently on the pedestals when the flying saucer lifted open and Shore entered climbing up the stairs before walking across the shiny white floor and positioning himself at the workstation. He began to operate the workstation which caused different frequencies of light to beam through Charlie and Jason which left them screeching in agony.

The lines on the, Shore's face represented the immense knowledge that he was currently absorbing; the results concluded every organ in Charlie and Jason's body, whilst Mimi continued to hide behind the pillar watching keenly.

Shore looked to a large screen where another alien appeared that began to communicate with him.

"Prior I have concluded my test they need energy in the form of food and water for their existence on planet Earth." Shore said.

"Shore I have concluded the same.' Prior replied and the alien continued to communicate via the large screen.

"We will exhibit them to the media tomorrow! Earthlings cannot exist in this kingdom without food or water. We must feed them." Prior informed whilst Shore listened intently before absorbing more knowledge via the computer:

"They have reproductive organs; life can continue, but they need a female to mate. These are of the same sex!" He continued.

"Once they are destroyed we can exhibit them in the museums their organs must be preserved so our future generations can see what earthlings are made from." Prior said leaving Mimi outraged by his intention.

"Do you know how rich we can become; we will be promoted to the highest seniors in space." He continued before the two aliens laughed uncontrollably previous to Prior vanishing of the screen and Shore leaving.

Mimi immediately returned to the workstation disarming the beam which allowed Jason and Charlie to jump off the pedestal.

"I have a plan you must fly out of here. The only way they can trap you is through the light energy. Keep out of the light." Mimi warned as Jason and Charlie flew towards the opening of the flying saucer.

"Charlie let's get the hell out of here!' Jason shouted.

Charlie smiled and then they both thanked Mimi before exiting out of the flying saucer towards the universe.

They were gliding around the stars and planets when they noticed the Journey Train, which had the words "Station" written by the stars.

They flew towards it then began to check the carriage windows before banging at the window where Scott and Linda slept. Luck meowed frantically at their presence at the window alerting Scott and Linda who immediately opened the window to let them in.

Linda and Scott were delighted when they arrived and immediately assisted them by hauling them through the window.

CHAPTER 13

Mystery Stop

They all relaxed in the train whilst the train carried on its journey speeding through planets, stars and darkness.

Then from time to time the steam cleared off the windows revealing all the different places, eras and people from around the world. The rows of streets in London were a familiar sight to Linda and Scott which they viewed excitedly when they appeared clearly visible through the window. There were historic buildings that were recognizable to them as they pointed at Westminster Abbey, Big Ben and the Eiffel Tower when they appeared; there were scenes of country lanes and woodlands with grand houses then there were views of Egypt with great kings alongside the pyramids. Many different feature and eras were displayed.

Charlie watched with great interest, when the Caribbean beaches and remote villages in Africa alongside the resident's in their traditional African costumes. The train speeded up and moved on to display the Sahara desert then continued through planets that were million's of light years away leaving them all sound asleep before the Journey Train came to a halt.

It seemed as if they visited every corner of the world and relived every century since the world began when a loud voice came through the speaker:

"Could all passengers terminate here this train terminates here; those wishing to continue their journey must board the next available train".

Sleepy heads awakened throughout the train peering through the window at the lake of fires, rocks, woodlands and red sand as the train pulled into the platform leaving all the passengers puzzled by the current destination. The train sped off as soon as the last passenger departed.

All the passengers followed signs that directed them outside to the huge black gates.

Once outside the crowds were mesmerized by intense heat caused by a volcanic eruption that left lakes of larvae deposited all around.

Soldiers, fire-fighter, police officers, teachers, pupils, mothers, fathers and children all found themselves roaming the red sands when panic and mayhem struck.

There was barking and howling coming from beast dogs alongside battalions of creatures resembling huge rats on horsebacks equipped with rifles and bayonet dressed in red tunics, red trousers and red helmets. They appeared charging at the passengers leaving them at the mercy of the two-headed dogs that growled and howled at the crowds. There was complete mayhem when soldiers mounted on horsebacks with cages and carts swung their whips and lashed out at the people who found themselves surrounded by the canine monsters with white creamy venom dripping from the corners of their mouth as the troops threw large nets to capture and place the crowds into carts and cages.

Linda Scott, Jason and Charlie ran frantically through the woodlands desperate to escape the beast dogs.

"Run!" Charlie screamed when the growling from the dogs got louder as they ventured deeper through the woodlands as a weak and tired Scott stopped to rest:

"My legs are tired!" Scott screeched ahead of Jason dragging him up.

"Keep running darling, you mustn't stop!" Linda shouted to him.

Scott kept running whilst Linda continued to shout at him every time she noticed him slowing down ahead of her.

"Keep running, darling the best dogs will get us" She reiterated before Jason stopped to put Scott on his back whilst the beast dogs growled as they continued running them down.

"In here, in here!" Charlie shouted he found a cave camouflaged with sticks which they all rushed towards. Jason tore his jacket wrapped it around a stone and then he flung it to send the beast dogs of track.

Only their eyes were visible and the sounds of heavy breathing as they all sat huddled and deflated in the blackness of the cold damp cave.

They were aware that they could not sit in the caves forever then Jason stood up and peeped outside.

"What if beast dogs are in here?" Scott asked.

Linda shook her head and then stood up.

"I don't think they are here." She said.

"What if the evil soldiers came back?" Scott asked clearly worried by the experience.

"I am going to see if the coast is all clear." Jason said leaving Linda worried for his safety.

"It may not be safe yet!" Linda said.

"We can't stay here forever." Jason replied as he walked outside the entrance.

Charlie was puzzled he did not want Jason to go out alone, but knew they must leave the cave.

"Listen I say we all stick to together here!" Charlie suggested.

Everyone agreed when suddenly Scott became very white before going into a sudden panic:

"Did you hear that?" He screeched leaving them listening keenly there it was again the sound of rustling noises behind them.

"The beast dogs are here!" Charlie shouted before dashing for the exit.

"Wait I don't think it's a beast dog; Listen!" Linda said.

They all listened intensively at the rustling of tiny footsteps comming closer.

"What is it?" Scott asked.

"I don't think it's the beast dog either!" Jason said.

CHAPTER 14

Salmon

The small footsteps continued to walk towards them whispering and rattling through the leaves in the caves.

They all continued towards the exit of the cave before noticing the cave get brighter.

There in front of them appeared an unusual man with a long fishtail, little legs and arms he had a small fish head with piecing wide green eyes.

He appeared harmless, but for the blazing torchlight which he carried. They were unsure about him because he was not recognizable to them he looked like a fish, but his face was very human like.

"Hello" Linda said, but the only response she got was him staring with stinging green eyes.

"You speak English?" She asked.

Linda got no reply to her question as she stared back at him with her stinging deep blue eyes.

He continued to walk towards her then relieving every one's suspicions about him he said:

"Yes, I speak many languages." He was softly spoken as he continued to edge towards them leaving them stunned by his appearance.

He walked over to Linda and touched her face and then he touched all their faces this was the fish man's way of welcoming them.

Come he gestured with his hands and they all followed him deeper into the cave with only the torch light to lead them through the darkness.

Suddenly they arrived at a stairway beneath some bushes which he cleared before the fish-man ordered them to follow him as he walked down the stairway which led to a stream with bright red spots that bubbled and smoked leaving them extremely amazed.

The fish man whistled which signalled for more fish men to arrive paddling towards them in boats which they all boarded.

The boats carried them deeper through the tunnel. Jason held on to the sides of the boat in a panic because the boat slowly began to disappear beneath the stream. He screamed at Linda who was tucking Luck safely in her bag before grabbing the sides of her boat that was sinking.

There were bubbles everywhere as all the boats vanished from the surface of the stream leaving them all confused by their abilities when realizing they were able to breathe under the waters.

"Look we can breathe under the water were not designed that way" Bellowed Jason before the canoes gathered together for them all to listen to the fish man.

"Salmon, my name is, Salmon." He said as he introduced himself properly to them.

"There is no need to fear me!" There are a lot more things you will fear before you come to the end of your journey. You will be safe in Fish Kingdom where fishes reside. I will give you the tools that will prepare you to overcome all the obstacles that await you boarding your train." Salmon said.

Everyone was bewildered by how knowledgeable Salmon was; he appeared to know so much about them.

The small boats continued to gather whilst Salmon continued to speak:

"You will breath in waters this may seem peculiar to you that's because you are getting your energy from a different source now" 'Salmon explained.

They continued to breathe under the silver stream as the canoes continued to take them deeper into the depths of the caves. They soon noticed the streams getting shallow allowing them to climb through a tunnel mounted in a wall under the stream.

All the water cleared when they reached the end of the tunnel and the silver stream appeared high above them as they floated towards the land welcomed by the residents waving and cheering.

Once they landed all the fish people followed behind them as they were led through there unusual kingdom to a beautiful sandy beach where they rested staring at the bright, red spots bubbling on top of them whilst they feasted on food and drinks.

They all sat around open fires very appreciative for the immense care and welcome they were shown by the residents as they continued to eat.

Jason looked at Charlie who was enjoying his food.

"What a place?" He said.

"It looks like it's some sort of Fish Kingdom." Charlie replied with Linda nodding in agreement.

"These are not ordinary fishes they are highly intelligent species" Jason said.

Salmon, had been listening keenly to the conversation.

"You are all very civil! We have met some humans before whilst on our missions to other kingdoms." Salmon informed.

They all continued to listen to Salmon.

"Where are you heading?" Salmon, asked.

"We are trying to get back to our kingdom Earth." Charlie told him.

"Oh." Salmon was looking surprised and remained silent for a brief moment.

"That's a very difficult mission because you will encounter many dangers. Not many make it back to Earth, but some do!" He said before he gestured an eye and then continued.

"That cave was very dangerous, because the evil rat men are always patrolling that area; many passengers that exit the train are captured by the rat men, who parole the stations and the entire kingdoms. If they do not take you by force they will bribe you throughout your mission by giving you food and wine and then they will tempt you away from Earth when they have converted you into evil people. You will never be welcomed into the kingdom of Cloudland, nor will you continue your journey to Earth.

Do not worry too much you are not far from Cloudland where your relatives will look after you. Salmon said.

That night they feasted on the finest wines until they were merry and then they rocked the night away under the red night surrounded by beautiful fishes.

Scott played football with the young fishes that picked him up and carried him each time he scored a goal while Linda relaxed in the company of lady fishes painting her nails and dressing her in glamorous garments whilst, Luck was happy to sleep through all the excitement.

They had enjoyed the previous night immensely when they awoke in the grand hotel with the sun shining through the window and the aroma of a hot breakfast.

Just as they were finishing their breakfast Salmon joined them at the breakfast table and they chatted for a while before Salmon announced: "You all need to follow me there are things you will need to continue your mission!"

He led them to his car and they were driven to a large castle high on a hill; they all followed Salmon up a large twisting staircase that led to a room that was filled with aerospace, shuttle equipment and computers configured around the walls.

Beneath the computers were worktops and chairs where they all sat.

Salmon operated the workstation which caused all the computers to display images of the universe. He then retrieved a wand from his desk that he used to point out the different planets appearing on the screen; at that moment Luck then decided to jump out of Linda's bag and bolted through the door. Linda and Salmon chased after him, but by the time she had reached the spiral staircase he had disappeared out of sight.

"Don't worry he'll come back." Salmon said while leading her back to her chair. He then familiarise them with all the planets that was visible on the computers before taken them to a window at the back of the room. On looking out they could see many different planets positioned million of light years away and then they noticed Earth orbiting around the sun.

"Wow" Scott said' He was truly amazed that everything seemed so near through the window when in reality the human eye could never witness these planets.

They were all gob smacked as they stood staring at the stars and planets that was clearly visible to them.

"We have to go to planet Nubeera to retrieve the tools that will equip you for your journey, but it is not free from danger. Some planet's we are able to enter because of their entry system, but other's have limited access; we can only enter them through specific conditions i.e. Being born into them and spiritual entry via the Journey Train, but this planet's will allow us to absorb entry."

Salmon paused to sip a glass of water and then splashed the remains all over him, before he continued.

"This mission is a dangerous one, but if you are to stand any chance in your quest to return to your lives it's a mission I think is vital." Salmon explained and they all nodded in agreement. As soon as Salmon opened the window a gust of wind blew them over. Salmon stepped outside adjusting his back pack secured tightly tis back then extending his tiny hands that were used as wings to float freely amongst the stars.

"Come he gestured with his hands to them. Charlie immediately followed his instruction only to find himself screaming frantically because he was falling uncontrollably.

"Help me!" He screamed.

Everyone watched helplessly through the open window as he began to float further away. Salmon gestured again for them to follow him, but they were reluctant after seeing what had happened to Charlie until he appeared floating towards them.

"This is fun!" He shouted as he floated around happily dancing and singing around the stars which encouraged them to jump through the window and join him.

They floated around merrily until they grew tired it wasn't long before they all glided around the universe when Salmon pointed at the planet they were about to enter in a bid to retrieve powerful tools, that would guard them throughout their mission to return to Earth.

He paraded around the planet that was moving rapidly in a circular motion.

"This is planet Nubeera it's also orbiting the Sun. Salmon stood himself beside the planet and waited for them to join him.

"There are dangerous inhabitants here we must be very careful" Salmon warned.

"I thought Earth was the only planet to orbit the Sun" Charlie questioned.

"Space is a big place there are many Sun's in space, some are millions of light years away! Are you all ready to enter?" Salmon asked before squashing himself against the planet until he was absorbed through to the other side.

CHAPTER 15

The Giant

Like a sponge absorbing water they were all absorbed into planet Nubeera; once they entered the planet they found themselves falling rapidly before their golden wings appeared which broke their fall, allowing them to glide through the skies.

They glided through the skies with Salmon whose hands had extended into wings which he used to glide towards huge trees that towered over huge castles. They continued to glide above the trees until they arrived at an enormous leaf where they rested for a while before continuing to fly.

"Why is everything so big?" Linda asked.

Salmon twitched an eyelid and then replied: "The inhabitants are large."

At that moment a loud thumping noise caused them to cover their ears.

"What is that?" Linda screeched.

Everyone nodded ahead of finding themselves positioned huddled in an alcove inside a tree trunk and pecking at them with its huge wing claw was a gigantic bird that roared and then pushed them all over.

The dinosaur squawked wildly when he realized they had all disappeared into the tree trunk continuing to fall rapidly through the tree.

"Err . . ." They screamed before opening their golden wings, which immediately broke their fall and glided them towards the bottom of the tree.

Once Salmon broke out of the tree he was determined to retrieve the magic mercury that was the last components needed for the tools that would enable them to complete their mission.

"We shall rest for a while then we will proceed to the caves to find the mercury." He said as they all stood bamboozled by their surroundings.

Linda was observing the huge trees, flowers and plants around her when she became baffled as soon as she stumbled across strange trees with identical tree trunks that were a peculiar pale colour. She became even more puzzled when looking down to the foot of the tree appeared a foot. Then she suddenly felt herself zoom off the ground to come face to face with a huge face peering at her.

She screamed loudly which alerted Scott and her friends who came running to her aid, but was defenceless against the huge giant who held her gently.

"Put her down!" Scott screamed, but it was in vain the giant did not see or hear him; he was besotted with his new find and had already taken a gigantic step which shook the ground like an earthquake causing them to tumble over and leaving them miles away from him.

The giant arrived at his castle surrounded my huge trees and large wild weeds he climbed the huge staircase holding Linda delicately before entering and closing the door behind him.

Linda was placed in a large, long, glass tube on a huge wooden table while the giant sat watching her banging the glass.

Beneath huge plants Salmon bombarded with questions from Jason, Charlie and Scott who was trying to mastermind a plan for Linda's safe return. Scott was devastated about what had happened to his mother despite Jason assuring him that Linda would be fine.

"We must first locate which castle she was taken too." Jason insisted.

"How do we even know she was taken to a castle or if she is still alive?" Charlie asked.

Jason shook his head which left them all silent as they became extremely worried about Linda.

"We must not give up hope! I am certain that she will return safely." Salmon said.

"How can you be so sure Salmon?" Jason asked he remained calm throughout, but when he realized he had no answers for Scott he raised his voice loudly at Salmon demanding an explanation. Charlie also began to demonstrate anger towards Salmon who had brought them to this forsaken place.

"How do we even know that Linda is still alive?" Charlie shouted.

By now Salmon could not contain his anger he became extremely frustrated.

"You blame me for Linda's misfortunes?" Salmon asked.

Charlie and Jason looked over to Scott who sat quietly longing for his mother's return; they gave Salmon an angry glare.

"Hey, guys, I had to bring you here! You have to get the tools for your mission! Your journey would be useless this is the only planet which has the mercury to activate your tools." Salmon stood his ground, but they were still not convinced by what he had said and they all continued to look at him waiting for him to come up with a solution.

"Linda will be safe for a while, we must go to the caves and retrieve the mercury and then we will try to rescue her." He suggested.

Jason was not happy with his suggestion and continued to demonstrate anger towards him.

"No, I say we rescue Linda first!" He insisted.

Salmon knew Jason was not happy, but he still tried to convince him that getting the mercury then rescuing Linda was the best solution.

"You cannot go near the inhabitants you will be eaten!" He said with his voice lightly raised.

"So how is Linda safe?" Charlie questioned exquisitely.

"Because the giants adore the daughter's of men and despise the sons of men. Trust me Linda will be fine." Salmon confirmed.

Scott was relieved to hear that his mother was not in any real danger before immediately standing beside Salmon.

"Salmon's our friend he's always been true to us, why doubt him now?" Scott said leaving them all looking at Salmon ashamed of their sudden outburst. Salmon quickly responded aware it was the right moment to regain full control of the situation.

"I know you are all very concerned about Linda, but we are the ones in real danger. If we are captured by the giants we will be eaten for sure; let's get the mercury and then tackle the giants." Salmon suggested more confidently.

Golden wings spread open as they cruised above castles, trees, over oceans and seas until they arrived at a small cave positioned beside the sea. Salmon immediately searched inside for the mercury with them all assisting; despite intensive searching throughout the water filled, damp cave they were unable to retrieve the mercury, this resulted in them deciding to leave the cave when Salmon stopped to study a large rock, which he later removed scrapings from and placed safely in a container.

Once he had enough of the substances he retrieved a map that he studied for a while ahead of them leaving the cave.

They arrived on the roof of a large castle where they sat watching a family of giants roaming around the castle grounds. The young giants played happily on huge swings whilst the parents sunbathed on chairs outside.

"Remember we must avoid all contacts with the giants." Salmon warned making them aware of the dangers they would encounter on their mission to rescue Linda from the clutches of the giant. There was no response from Scott, his face was a reminder of a lost soul desperate for his mother's safe return which made Salmon more determined for Linda's safe return.

They all flew towards the tower of the castle and with great difficulty prized open the window. Once inside they noticed a large table with enormous knives and forks, huge salt and pepper containers alongside gigantic cups and plates.

A huge wind slowly filled the room which caused them to roll along the windowsill, when the breeze stopped they rushed for refuge inside the plates; the wind blew strongly again leaving Scott unable to reach the plate it whisked him like a feather across the table into the pathway of the spikes of the fork he screamed loudly. He closed his eyes fearing he was about to be stabbed by a gigantic spike. When the wind stopped and allowed him to dash into the plate with his friends. They remained inside the plate for a short time before deciding what they should do.

"We must not remain here, if the giants return we will be eaten!" Salmon said.

"I agree we don't want to remain on this plate." Jason said with sarcasm.

"When the wind stops blowing we will have to fly out and try to make our way over to the shelves." Salmon said as he pointed to the huge shelves secured to the wall with books and ornaments.

"It will be a lot safer there." Jason confirmed in full agreement with Salmon.

The breeze stopped blowing and they all tried to fly over to the shelves, but it started again leaving Scott and Charlie up against the pepper containers whilst Salmon was left holding on to the rim of the plate and Jason left holding a splinter on the edge of the table; he looked below him to find he was higher from the ground than a mountain; he then felt his hands slipping along the splinter. "Help!" he shouted as he was about to let go, but his wings just flapped uncontrollably in the breeze causing him to hold the splinter tighter, which slowly began to break away.

The wind stopped, this relieved him of his fears and enabled him to fly over to the shelves where his friends joined him. When the breeze continued it knocked over flowerpots and blew over many items on the shelves which left them huddled beside the huge book.

Salmon looked to see where the breeze was coming from becoming startled as he peered through an ajar door to reveal a snoring, open, mouthed giant fast asleep on an enormous bed.

"We must not disturb him." Salmon whispered as they all flew across the room quietly searching cupboards and draws for Linda.

Exhausted from the search they threw themselves onto what appeared a large, fluffy rug, where they became overwhelmed by a large deafening, howling noise as they felt themselves being raised about six feet above the ground.

They grabbed hold of the fluffy strands of wool to be shaken vigorously ahead of landing in a large pool that left them swimming to the edge. Confronting them was a huge, shaggy dog that towered above them with his tongue hanging ready to lap up the water; he then noticed them and barked wildly awakening the giant who immediately jumped up. On the vibration of his movement it left them scattered around the floor in puddles of water; on him remaining still for a few moments they were able to fly to the shelves and take refuge amongst the flowerpots, but the giant had seen them; he threw the flowerpot off the shelves to reveal them standing trembling, wet and petrified. He banged his fist missing them by a whisker; this resulted in them becoming thrust around every corner of the room where the giant stood waiting with a large bowl of flour that sunk them like quick sand coughing and choking as they were rescued by the giant himself; he picked them out one by one and placed them on the table still covered in white powder, then they were cleaned and placed in a huge open container. The giant was about to pick up the container, but he heard a loud audible sound echoing throughout the castle, there was somebody at the door. The giant left the room.

"The window" Salmon shouted knowing there was not a moment to spare as they all flew through the window leaving the dog barking loudly.

"That was close." Jason said as they rested on the twig of a huge tree.

"Yes a bit too close for comfort" Salmon said looking extremely worried.

"We need to leave this planet very soon because the train will be arriving to take you to your next destination." He continued.

"We have got to find my mum." Scott said as they all nodded approvingly and immediately flew to another huge castle.

They entered the castle through an opened window where they stood reluctant to move because of what they had previously encountered. Then they noticed Linda she appeared happy and contented, she was wearing beautiful clothes and her hair was neatly combed as she laid relaxed and eating tiny pieces of fruit.

"My mum" Scott shouted he was enlightened to see her alive and well and they immediately flew over to her.

"Hello" She said as she hugged and greeted them before they all helped themselves to the fresh fruits.

"We have to leave immediately, or you risk missing the train and your Earth Time could run out." Salmon warned.

"Ok let's get out of here before the giant returns." Linda warned.

They flew over mountains and valleys, then high into the clouds before exiting the planet to arrive back at the aerospace room.

Salmon positioned in front of the workstation holding his wand tightly whilst retrieving a pair of glasses fitted on to the scales either side of his head pointed at the screen. "The equator, that imaginary horizontal line at zero degrees latitude at the centre of the Earth divides the Earth into the northern and southern hemisphere. This is Earth situated on the northern hemisphere" Salmon explained whilst pointing his wand at the different images that became visible on the screen.

"The only way for you to reach Earth is by the Journey Train; you probably rode on it before." He took a deep sigh and then adjusted his glasses before he continued in a high-pitched voice.

"Forces are very important. You see forces fuse together and generate magnetic fields. We are all products of the magnetic force all around the orbit.

We are all journeying to everlasting life. Our planets will end when its relevant journey as come to an end and matter dissolves.

Our souls are molecules waiting for some force or attraction to which are compatible with our matter will fuse and take up life as we know it, we will become the energy force that controls the attraction." He said as he placed his wand down and raised his eyebrow to continue.

"This is very complicated because you are all human energy's trying to return to your homes which are situated on Earth otherwise known to be souls.

You keep your human image, but your force, your soul is what makes your identity."

Everyone listened intensely to Salmon he was silent for a while before he gasped for air then he looked at each of them adjusting his glasses.

"Now the evil rat men are out there to destroy your souls. You will become the servants of the rat men if captured. You must return you to the Journey Train, but armed. If you come into any contact with evil, you must rebuke them. If your souls are pure you will arrive in Cloudland, and then continue your journey through Red Fire and then return to Earth, your destiny will be in your hands alone."

Everyone was left dumbfounded by what Salmon told them while there eye's remained fixed on Salmon's movements as they watched him open his draw to retrieve four laser pens. He activated a button on one of the lasers and a long green beam shone onto a metal object which sliced into two pieces.

"This laser is very powerful. If you shine from range it has the ability to decapitate its victim." He said while pushing down on the pen top which released an aching noise that caused them to cover their ears.

"This noise will repel any animal away from you." He said handing the pens to each of them; he fumbled again in his draw this time he pulled out some chewing gum which he gave them.

"You humans love to chew well this will keep you cool whenever you are dehydrating. Chew one of these and you will be able to tolerate extreme heat!"

They were then given a watch with black waterproof straps attached was an egg timer across the face.

"Inside here is the magic mercury that we retrieved from planet Nubeera this will alert you when there is a train in the vicinity more important it shows your Earth Time if you click on this button." Salmon demonstrated by clicking on the button before explaining the device further.

"If your watch alarms it will warn you that you are very low on Earth Time when there are no signals remaining, you must be on the Journey Train to Earth. You will lose your Earth Time and all connections if you run out of signal strength." He continued to explain leaving them troubled at the fact that it was possible they could lose all connections with Earth.

"Currently you all have Earth Time, but do not abuse your times; your Earth Time can be reduced without warning so be sure to check your signal strength; finally I will return you all to the cave tomorrow and you will have to board the Journey Train." He said while being interrupted by something licking and pulling his leg.

Linda, was embarrassed when she saw, Luck looking as if he was about to have his supper, she quickly grabbed him and ushered him into her bag.

CHAPTER 16

Exiting Fish Kingdom

Salmon was a very wise fish that equipped them with the tools that were essential in their battles to return to their life on Earth prior to warning them of the dangers that they would encounter on their mission.

Fish Kingdom was an unusual place, where residents continued with their everyday lives.

Many different types of fishes were amongst the residents who were shopping for clothing, computers, furnishing and many other items; they all stopped what they were doing when distracted by the humans that walked through the city with Salmon.

"Humans are thought of very highly in Fish Kingdom. Salmon explained whilst they all listened intensely, he spoke about his kingdom with pride as he talked about the fate of the codfishes:

"The cod fish believed that humans ate fish, that's why they are no longer welcome in Fish Kingdom we all believe humans are kind to fishes on Earth."

They all remained silent joined by thousands of fishes who marched behind them playing trumpets, drums whilst chanting songs before they arrived back at the beach.

It was a very sad day because they were leaving Fish Kingdom. They boarded one of the many clouds ahead of them waving goodbye to the fish people.

Fish kingdom began to fade with the waving residents becoming mere specs whilst the silver stream was in full view ahead of them.

Salmon waved them goodbye when they approached the entrance of the cave leaving them much aware of the dangers that was ahead of them still intrigued about the kingdom they just left.

"What a beautiful place that was" Jason said as they continued paddling in the small boats back through the cave.

"Salmon was a highly intelligent fish!" Linda said amazed by his wisdom.

Then there was beeping Salmon's image appeared on the faces of the watches:

"Be aware of the evil rat men they parole the stations and land; remember they will try to bribe you by giving you food, wine and tempt you away from your mission; when they have converted you into their people you will never be welcomed into the kingdom of Cloudland or be allowed to continue your journey to Earth." Salmon then pointed to a monitor.

"You are on a dangerous mission. You must be aware of all the danger you may encounter; you are not far from Cloudland where you will meet your past relative, you will be safe for a while.

This is Earth situated in the northern hemisphere. There are two entries into earth to be born or via the Journey Train; remember we are all products of the magnetic force all around the orbit.

Some of us will journey to everlasting life, before the planets end, but usually our lifespan matter will dissolve before then.

Our souls are molecules waiting for some force or attraction to which are compatible with matter to fuse then we take up life as we know it. We become the energy force that controls the attraction.

All complicated stuff; you are all human energy trying to return to your energy homes which is situated on Earth.

You will keep your human image, but your force, your soul is what makes your identity.

The evil rat men are out there to destroy your souls. You will become the servants of evil if you follow their ways.

You must always try to return to the Journey Train. If you come into any contact with the evil rat men you must rebuke them. If your souls are pure you will be destined for life and will continue your journey to the destination that you have known. However there are many distractions and forces you will have to overcome." Salmon said as he faded away and the watches switching off.

The pre-recording was a reminder of the important facts that Salmon did not want them to forget.

CHAPTER 17

Arriving in Cloudland

Jason was not convinced about all that Salmon had said when Linda became aware that Scott was clearly missing Salmon,

"When we get home Scott I will get you some fishes." Linda promised as she tried to charm him hoping to cheer him up, but he was not impressed.

"No I don't want any! Scott replied.

"I thought you were fond of fishes, you liked Salmon . . . Didn't you?" Linda asked.

"I don't want any fishes to be enslaved by me they belong in the oceans. They belong in Fish Kingdom!" Scott shouted angrily. Linda smiled and nodded in agreement:

"Your right darling I always took fishes for granted, but I guess meeting Salmon it's taught me a few things."

"I will never eat fish again." Scott announced.

Their watches alerted them that they needed to get back to the station to board the train.

They were reluctant when leaving the cave because they feared the evil rat men were about to attack them when they were reminded about their tools by Jason which encouraged them to continue their journey?

They walked through the red sand in a single file towards the station when they noticed everywhere deserted unlike the crowded scenes that they had met before.

On arriving at the station the evil rat men galloped towards them fiercely. Charlie searched each pocket before retrieving his laser.

"The soldiers are here!" Jason shouted, when noticing them coming towards them at full speed.

"Shine the beam!" Charlie ordered as he activated his laser dismounting some of them.

Jason immediately shone his beam which caused the horses to whimper before galloping away. Linda and Scott activated their lasers whilst charging at the soldiers this allowed them to gain access to the station entrance.

Once inside the station they were met by snarling and growling beast dogs. Scott went forth and shone his laser which caused the two headed beast dogs to back away thus allowing them to enter the station platform, where they boarded the waiting train.

"All Passengers destined for Cloudland please board the train" was the message echoed throughout the station.

The train doors closed leaving the evil rat men parading around the station gates with the dusty, red sand blowing freely in the breeze.

The train sped through the clouds and over the stars, then around the planets whilst they all slept soundly.

They had been sleeping for a few hours when they were woken by a loud voice coming through the speakers announcing they would be arriving in Cloudland shortly.

They had no idea how long they were sleeping, but was very excited to be arriving safely in Cloudland.

Everyone was fully awakened by the message "All Passengers please exit the train" that played continuously as the train pulled into Cloudland station.

They noticed the beautiful white doves that flew beside the window as they proceeded towards the train doors where passengers queued to depart the train; whilst queuing Scott noticed the distinctive white gowns with huge golden wings that were being worn by the staff on board the train's that cared for small children and babies.

CHAPTER 18

Magdalene

They were dumbfounded when they arrived at the main hall to see so many people standing around holding placards; one read: "Aunty Mavis comes to collect Sean Anise."

They continued to walk through the hall when Scott was excited to see a placard with his name:

"I am looking for Linda Harris & Scott Harris." Scott alerted his mum whilst pointing to the placard. "Look Mum" Scott shouted.

Linda immediately turned to notice the board and then noticed her grandmother and raced over to her:

", Nana" She shouted which was often the name she used to address her grandmother, who turned around immediately.

"Linda" she replied as their eyes filled with tears whilst they stared at each other gathering thoughts and fond memories.

"I've missed you so much" Linda said as the fond memories surfaced on her mind:

The autumn leaves on the tall trees tossed to and fro falling to the ground one by one a little girl who raced back to her tricycle and picked up a leaf.

Linda was often seen riding her bike in the park with her grandfather, George. George a middle aged man would run behind the tricycle clutching his hat to stop the strong breeze blowing it away whilst Magdalene a beautiful middle aged woman stood laughing, because she knew the wind would always get it.

Magdalene often grabbed Linda from her tricycle throwing her in the air whilst George picked up the tricycle and they all walked home.

Her thought's then drifted to the last day spent with her grandmother; she recalled a nine year old girl returning from school to be met by her grandfather walking down the stairs. When he approached her she noticed the tears and sorrow in his eyes as her mother came out of the kitchen and hugged him.

"I think she's ready to go now" George cried leading Linda into the room where her grandmother was still on the bed.

"Gran-mother" Linda shouted as she rushed towards her climbing onto her bed to lie beside her; she remembered her grandmother stroking her hair with weak trembling hands.

"I must leave you all! How I'm going to miss my little angel." she muttered struggling to utter her words.

"Where are you going?" Linda asked as she curled up beside her and felt her weakness trying to comfort her. She waited for a response from her that never arrived before falling soundly asleep beside her. She dreamt about high clouds above large golden gates with little golden angels playing harps as she walked up the huge staircase with her grandmother; the gates parted on their arrival.

"This is where I am going! My angel here is where I must leave you!" Her grandmother said.

"I want to come too!" Linda begged prior to her grandmother picking her up and swinging her around.

"I will be with you each step of the way like you were with me climbing those steps. I will be with you throughout your life until we meet again." She continued.

Linda remembered her kissing her cheek before her mother waking her.

Linda was amazed by how ageless and youthful Magdalene looked. She had a bright smile that Linda only recognized from photographs. Magdalene turned to Scott. "You must be Scott." She said.

Scott smiled and they both embraced.

"I know all about you! I'm Magdalene your great, great grandmother." She told him, before breaking the embrace. Linda was eager to introduce her friends to her grandmother and immediately grabbed her arm.

"Grandmother this is Charlie and Jason my friends." She said as Magdalene shook their hands respectively and introduced herself.

Linda checked inside her bag and Luck, popped his head out.

"Oh, this is Luck." She said.

Magdalene smiled at the quiet black cat inside Linda's bag before turning to Jason and Charlie with a concerned look:

"Have you met any of your relatives yet?" She asked and they both shook their heads,

"We must try and find them." Magdalene insisted before wandering through the crowds reading the placards. There were many people waiting patiently for relatives and friends, but they could not find anyone who was connected to Jason or Charlie,

The aroma of coffee beans brewing tempted them to enter the coffee bar before being seated at a small, round table with green cushions neatly on the wooden benches. They were drinking coffee and chatting amongst themselves when two young women approached them.

"Have you guys just come off the Cloudland train?" One asked.

They all looked at her and nodded. It was at that point Charlie immediately stood up:

"Sharon, Sharon." He said staring at her dark brown skin whilst admiring her silky black hair that was pulled firmly back before greeting each other with a warm hug.

"I forgive you" Sharon whispered whilst locked in his arms.

Charlie stared at Sharon; recollecting the memories they shared with his thoughts drifting to a hot sunny day with them both sat on benches at the fairground eating burgers and fries, whilst minding their child sitting in the pram. Charlie appeared handsome and strapping whilst, Sharon was youthful and happy.

They pushed the small child through the fairground before they stopped at the rifle stall, where Charlie tested his rifling skills, firing at the targets confidently and winning a small cuddly toy for his efforts. Sharon was spun around on the carousel whilst Charlie stood minding his child waving at her each time she appeared; it was a fun packed day and they had won many prizes before he remembered the darker times.

He sat at the table with a pile of unpaid bills whilst Sharon had found the food cupboard empty again then the baby screamed at her impatiently because she was due her next feed. He remembered staring at the ceiling when he was disturbed by a loud noise caused by Sharon throwing the pots out of the cupboard, before kicking the kitchen door then approaching Charlie in a rage:

"You're useless; you're absolutely useless! I'm sick of this absolutely sick of it, Charlie!" Sharon shouted with the baby in one arm and her bag on the other.

"I'm leaving and you won't see me or your baby again!" She shouted.

Charlie raced after her pleading with her to come back, but the door slammed he rushed to the window to see her speed away. He phoned her continuously for months, but her phone was always off then years later her mother rang him and informed him of the devastating news there was a house fire and Sharon and his child were unable to escape. These were the last memories he had of Sharon. He returned from his thought and noticed everyone watching them admiringly; he was confused why did, Sharon come to meet him? She had no right to come here, her love was lost years ago and why had she forgiven him, when he could never forgive her for taken his child away.

Charlie put his thoughts aside and introduced Sharon to his friends:

"This is Sharon the mother of my daughter, Jane they were both killed in a fire." Charlie announced.

His friends felt sad for him as they witnessed the sorrow that overcame him they knew this must have been a very traumatic time in his life.

"This is Jane!" Sharon said leaving Charlie taken aback he did not recognize the young girl beside her and was pleased to see his daughter who had grown into a beautiful young lady that was a far cry from the screaming toddler he once knew.

"I have missed you so much! I had so many plans for you!" He said hugging his long lost daughter.

"I have missed you too! Jane said delighted to see her father.

Charlie's mood changed to anger because his daughter was a stranger he had missed so much of her life. Why did Sharon do this? He thought.

Sharon noticed his anguish before explaining all the things that Jane had done:

"Jane's achieved very good grades at school and she was the captain of the netball team." she informed; knowing she could never undo the past.

Charlie wanted to relive those precious years, but knew it was all too late for that. He needed to explain to Jane that he was not planning to stay here, but it was hard for him because he feared upsetting her again. It was that moment when, Jane took his hand:

"Dad I want to take you somewhere" She said whilst leading him out of the station towards speeding clouds that came crashing directly at them. Charlie was left bamboozled in a strange place peering through the window of a classroom.

Inside, Jane sat working by her desk when she walked over to touch the window before smiling at him.

The classroom miraculously transformed into a netball pitch where Charlie and other parents gathered around watching the game that Jayne was participating in. Charlie feels proud when Jayne scores a goal then rushes over to the window to share her joy with him. She throws the ball at the window and then the netball match changes to a living room with a Christmas tree with festive decorations. Jayne is seen rushing down the stairs early Christmas morning to open her present whilst Charlie peers through the window at her discovering the bike she always wanted. She is seen riding her bike in the snow before leaving it and running over to Charlie.

"I hope these memories will ease the pain of you missing out on so much," Jayne whispers.

Charlie and Jayne, return to the station to join the others. They all finished their coffee when Jason began to worry because everyone was reunited with their families except him. Linda noticed how worried he looked:

"Don't worry! I am sure someone will be along shortly." She said which caused, Magdalene, to look over at her with a worried look in her eyes:

"I'm not so sure." She said looking at Sharon who nodded in agreement before they all stared at Jason.

"Everyone been reunited with their families if you haven't met up with your families they have not been notified of your arrival!" Magdalene continued she was very concerned.

"Can we contact them?" Linda asked?

Magdalene shook her head.

"No!" Jason is in the wrong place." She said.

"If Jason is in the wrong place surely we are all in the wrong place too?" Linda shouted which caused everyone to remain silent as she continued:

"We are trying to get back to Earth Nan it's not our time yet. Emily needs us. We don't want to stay in Cloudland?" Magdalene was stunned she looked at Sharon and then Jayne who mirrored her reaction.

"Why on Earth would you want to go back there? It is a lovely place Cloudland! You first have to discover Cloudland." Magdalene said as she tried to convince them to stay:

"Once you have seen what Cloudland's like, nobody gets the train to Red Fire and risk the journey back to Earth." Magdalene continued before taking a breath and looking at each of them.

"We only allow good people to come here. I don' know why Jason's relatives were not informed."

Jason continued to feel uneasy about what Magdalene had said. He then blurted out:

"I am a good person!" Everyone remained silent this caused him to lower his head ashamed of his outburst.

"I have done some bad things, but that shouldn't stop me coming here. I was young and I made mistakes I had no idea I would be an outcast in Cloudland." He said.

"I'm sorry, Jason truly I am there must be something we can do." Linda said at the same time looking over to her grandmother for a solution.

"Can Jason come with us?" Linda asked leaving Magdalene looking surprised.

"He'll be a fugitive! How absurd! Of course he can't! If they realize that we are harbouring a fugitive we will be punished as well." She said.

"This is Cloudland grandmother what happened to forgiveness?" Linda asked.

"We only allow good people in here!" Magdalene replied.

He is a friend! He saved us from the evil rat men! I will not leave him! I won't.!' Linda shouted.

Magdalene knew that Jason was a brave soldier and a hero to everyone, but was not convinced he was a good person as she looked at him again with suspicion.

"There is no compassion for cruel and evil people they are outcast! No one would accept him here." Magdalene said.

Linda was ashamed of her grandmother's bitter tongue towards her friend, her hero and someone she admired whilst Jason felt condemn and angry that he should be made to feel like a criminal.

"I'm not perfect. What man is? You have to believe me I'm not evil or wicked my heart is good. I'm a good person." He said as he protested his innocent.

Everyone started to show signs of suspicion towards him except Linda who still had faith in him although she had only known him for a short time. She knew he was brave and strong, but knew nothing about his family, or the man himself.

"I won't turn him in! We will all try to board the next train out of here together!" Linda insisted.

Magdalene knew she was determined to help her friend and agreed to help him on one condition.

"You must agree to visit the trees of wisdom." Magdalene said to him. Jason accepted her condition which left everyone sighing with relief.

It was time for Charlie to break the devastating news to Linda and Jayne who had already suspected he would not be around for long.

"I was happy to see you both. It's been very difficult for me not to be a part of my daughter's life," He said as Sharon stood holding Jayne's hand.

"We will miss you, I'm so sorry, Charlie! I hope you can forgive me." She said as she walked over and embraced him. Charlie smiled on pulling away from the embrace.

"We were young and foolish." He said before walking over to Jayne.

"The memories you gave me I will treasure forever." He said before wiping away tears whilst Jayne tiptoed and kissed him on the cheek.

CHAPTER 19

Wisdom Trees

The s taxi arrived at a place where the burning sun beamed down on the fields around them; they stepped out to be met by tall, unusual trees, long, green, grass with beautiful flowers spouting out of them while clear running water flowed through the stepping-stones positioned around the streams directly in front of them.

They all followed Magdalene who jumped across the stones to come face to face with some huge, colourful and unusual flowers with grey stems and beautiful purple, petals; the tall trees towered over them with trunks formed from human bodies and a head of different colour leaves attached to faces embedded in the trunks.

Magdalene stood in front of many tree's before deciding which one to pick.

"Every tree tells a story here because they are all trees of wisdom that is capable of revealing questions we request answers for, like why Jason was refused entry in to this kingdom and what we will need to do to keep him here?" Magdalene said. This left Linda annoyed with her grandmother because she was still convinced that they would remain in Cloudland.

"I keep telling you, but you refuse to listen! We do not want to stay here I was serious we need to go back to Earth. Our life's there is not over yet" She explained.

Magdalene was still convinced that Linda would change her mind once she had discovered what a beautiful place Cloudland was.

"Jason will need to find out what he must do he will be returning here one day and he will be faced with the same problem; if he's not welcomed here he will be doomed for Red fire."

She warned before looking up at a tree then rubbing the bark.

The tree awakened shaking its leaves as if it was its hair then the eyes opened and the whole tree came to life.

A deep male voice commanded Jason to step forward. A frightened Jason came forward while the rest of them stood back.

The tree took a deep breath and sighed before closing its eyes for a few moments then the eyes opened and he blew out a gash of air causing Jason to plunge to the floor.

"You seek answers why you are not welcomed in Cloudland. Earthly challenges still await you!" The tree said before closing its eyes.

Magdalene was not happy with what the tree said because she thought the tree had been very brief.

"We need to find a tree that can give us a bit more detail." She said rubbing a tree which awakened flicking its leaves and taking deep breaths and then breathing gashes of air. This time it was a kind soft voice that spoke.

"Jason should not be here. Someone has made a mistake. When the mistake is rectified he will return to his life on Earth." The tree closed its eyes.

Jason was now aware that he was in the wrong place however there were still questions he needed to know. How long would it take before the mistakes were rectified? What would happen if they were not rectified? Jason turned to another tree and rubbed it and the tree awakened.

The leaves shook vigorously, and then there was cracking of thunder and a loud roar. This tree was scary and spoke with sarcasm.

"We don't know the answers to outcomes however your destiny is in your hands now." The tree closed its eyes immediately.

Charlie was delighted that it was confirmed Jason's journey back to Earth would be worthwhile and he looked at Jason before assuring him:

"We are all heading in the same direction and we all want to return to our lives on Earth, Welcome abroad mate." He said before they shook hands.

Little stars twinkled in the sky when the dark night fell. Moving monuments were visible all around the cities, while large statues walked freely along the pavements before returning to the perches. Magdalene pointed out the moving lions that left their perches she knew them by name.

"There's, Harold and Ernie going for a stride." She said as they all peered through the taxi window in disbelief at the walking statues.

Linda decided they should all remain together until the train arrived and Magdalene convinced them all to come home with her until their train was ready to depart. They continued their journey through the well-lit cities amazed by the beautiful white buildings and low clouds surrounding them.

The taxi pulled up in front of the beautiful white gates that opened revealing 'Harris House,' a beautiful Elizabethan stately home surrounded by parkland, lakes fringed with beautiful trees.

A youthful man ran towards them waving vigorously as he approached. Linda stared hard at the familiar face that was full of glee and happiness when he saw her as Magdalene, stepped forward to announce: "Welcome to Harris House." Linda stood smiling still intrigued by the man in front of her. Magdalene noticed her confusion then apologized, before introducing them.

"George Harris my husband" she said grabbing George's arm whilst pulling him towards Linda who was now aware that the familiar face was her grandfather.

"Granddad, I've missed you so much!" She said throwing her arms around him.

She always remembered an old fragile man how handsome and fresh he looked. She wiped away the tears of joy unlike the tears she cried out of anguish and sorrow when he departed.

George smiled and greeted her then he greeted each of them, before leading them into the house.

"Come, Come, the food will go cold." He said as he lead them to a large dining room that was beautifully furnished and filled with merriness and joy there were clowns performing juggling and dancing acts. Golden platters and goblets dressed the table,

The food decorated with food paints whilst blackbirds hidden in the pies that flew out and amazed the guests.

Trumpets and drums accompanied with music and singing that complimented to the merriness and joy all around them as each dish was announced.

Luck finally got to escape the clutches of Linda's bag as he played merrily with a family of cats that were situated at the far end of the dining room whilst Scott played happily with his new found cousins, uncles and other family member's he was unaware of.

Some adults sat at the table drinking fine wine, while reminiscing about their Earth days whilst Jason and Linda explored the grounds surrounding Harris House.

There were beautiful woodlands and parklands, with a beautiful river between them.

They walked along the riverbank until they arrived at a boat. Stooping beside the disused wooden boat anchored to the bank Jason turned to Linda and said:

"I didn't get a chance to thank you earlier for your support" Linda smiled admiringly she knew it was becoming harder to hide the strong feelings she had for him. She remembered the outburst she displayed to her grandmother when it was thought Jason would not be allowed to enter Cloudland.

They stood in the beautiful parklands under the stars whilst the moon light beamed down upon them and they kissed.

Two tiny, ivory angels with golden, ringlets and beautiful, golden wings with a bow and arrow strapped to their backs flew around them.

Linda and Jason watched them in admiration. "They are cupids!" Linda announced then climbed into the boat with Jason and the cupids. An arrow then shot at the anchor which released the boat and allowed Jason to paddle down the river.

They paddled right out of the grounds of Harris House with the moon beaming down illuminating colourful fishes swimming in the still waters. Ahead of them they could see a large clouds hovering just above the river.

The cupids hovered on to a cloud before signalling for them to follow and they both jumped onto the hovering cloud with the cupids taken the controls.

The stars began to get bigger as they journeyed higher into the skies as Jason held Linda tighter; then the cupids left the controls causing the cloud to speed out of control into the path of a star which made them close their eye's fearing a crash, but the star door opened and they entered.

The cupids golden, wings and ringlets were most visible inside the star filled with thick, white mist. Hidden behind the mist were ivory doors that flung open when the cupids approached them.

Linda and Jason stood back in amazement when the doors flung open to reveal large, bubbles with people's faces inside.

Linda got closer to a bubble to discover Emily's face inside prior to the cupid's reaching for their arrow to pierce it. The arrow struck the bubble which burst into a thousand teardrops ahead of Linda immediately finding herself back home sitting at Emily's bedside stroking her hair as she lay asleep.

"Don't worry! Mummy and Scott will be home soon?" Emily was awakened by the aroma of her mother's perfume and the whisper of her voice which made her race into the next room to alert her grandmother.

"My mother was here! I heard her voice and smelt her perfume!" She explained with glee and happiness protruding from her face. Nanny White rubbed her eyes then looked at Emily then at the clock displaying three am.

"You're tired darling" Go back to bed!" She ordered; as Emily turned towards the door she shouted.

"You smelt her perfume?" Emily nodded.

"I believe you." she said as Emily quietly closed the door.

Nanny White knew she had found inner strength, hope and the belief that her mother and her brother would be coming home.

Linda returned immediately to witness the cupids piercing another bubble this time it was Jason's mother face that the arrow struck before the bubble shattered in to thousands tiny tears drops.

At that moment he was at home with his elderly mother, who sat heartbroken crying over his photographs beside an electric fire with a blanket whilst the family album lay open on the table. Jason walked over picking up a letter beside her that confirmed he was missing and feared dead.

His mother saw the disturbance when the letter floated in the air by itself as she looked on in disbelief whilst Jason hugged her and whispered that, he would be coming home.

His mother smiled then embraced his presence when hearing his voice.

Jason returned to the star to be ushered through another door. Inside there was lots of cupids floating above golden cradles that had the most beautiful new-born babies inside, that the cupids were highly protected over. Jason and Linda were led to the most beautiful baby in a cradle the only cupids that was seen at this cradle were the two with Linda and Jason. Linda had a peculiar thought as she turned to Jason and asked.

"What if it's our baby?"

This surprised Jason who was left gob smacked.

The word's Mother Nature was written on another door in golden letters when the door opened it revealed the most beautiful garden with deep, green grass fringed with beautiful large, bluebells, daffodils, beautiful lilies, roses and many more colourful flowers.

There were large, glass, tubes, with striking, enormous butterflies with large, velvet wings flying from them.

Jason and Linda sat on the grass where white doves tweeted around them before being joined by singing birds and bluebirds who sang then danced ahead of forming into beautiful hearts with the words Linda and Jason being added to the top and bottom respectfully then the cupids left one of its golden arrows across the heart. It was the most beautiful performance they ever witnessed before staring into each other's eyes lovingly, then sharing another kiss.

After leaving the beautiful garden they were back aboard the speeding cloud with the cupids at the controls as they sped into the night through the colourful, lit city.

The sound of loud music bellowed from the city when they dismounted the cloud. On arriving at the carnival there were sounds of laughter comming from the big wheel and many other attractions.

Jason and Linda rode on the bumper cars eating candyfloss then it was the carousel, before making a dash for the rollercoaster where they shrieked with laughter from spinning rapidly; then it was time to board the cloud again the cupids at the controls.

The next stop was blasting of music, but this time it was the sound of steel bands alongside live bands and sound system. They found themselves amongst revellers dressed in eccentric costumes dancing through the crowds whilst trying to see the beautiful, colourful, loud costumes parading on the streets and on floats.

There was so much to do and see they wanted to stay longer, but the cupid's insisted it was time to go.

The next stop was a town filled with large statues. Linda and Jason dismounted the clouds to be greeted by Harold and Ernie they were statues of lion's that were about to take them on a guided tour of the cities; ahead of the cupids waving them goodbye.

They were engulfed by the clowns performing on the streets and the street dancers on arriving at Children City; they flew over houses, parks and buildings; there were past children mounted on flying bird; as more pre historic birds played in harmony with children riding on their backs whilst some sat asleep on the open grass with lions, tigers and small cubs beside them.

Linda and Charlie astounded by how beautiful it was to see such gentleness from such fearful looking animals and birds, as they watched the children swinging on trees with monkeys and romping with lions and bears.

They jumped back onto Harold and Ernie and were flown back to the entrance of Harris House; as the lions rode off into the night.

Magdalene greeted them by the door when they arrived holding hands and staring into the night until the lions were out of sight.

They were happy in Cloudland because family, friends and love ones were all around which made it easy to forget about the world they once knew.

It was a beautiful sunny day and the sun beamed as the Harris family and their friends sat by the river enjoying the parkland surrounding of Harris House, when Scott's watch started to alarm alerting them that he was running out of Earth Time.

This made Linda extremely worried as she gasped at his watch whilst holding his hand tightly.

"He needs to board the next train if he's to stand any chance of returning to Earth and his former life." She warned.

The Journey Train would be arriving the following morning so they were all prepared to leave Harris House and collected the last of their belongings.

Luck, seemed very happy amongst the other cats and kittens it was difficult for Linda to uproot him she was not aware how much Earth Time he had remaining and did not want to risk losing him in Red Fire, so she decided to leave him with his new found friends.

Magdalene called a taxi to take them to the station whilst they all said their final goodbyes to all the members of the Harris household.

CHAPTER 20

Raging Jim

The strong breeze left Magdalene grabbing her hat and Linda cleared her hair from her face as the train pulled into the platform. This train was different from the last train it was unpainted with blacked out windows. It did not have cubicles just row of seats in carriages that had stoned floors, large pillars, and dim light fitments.

The train doors closed leaving them all feeling cold as they stood waving goodbye to Magdalene who waved whilst watching the train speed away.

Once inside the train they seated themselves on the cushioned seats all eyes focusing on the bland walls and damp, concrete floors and the emptiness throughout the carriages unlike the grand, packed carriages they had boarded before.

On checking the status of the signal strengths there was cause for concern because they were all low except Linda's that remained in a reasonable state.

"I wouldn't worry, we'll all make it!" Linda assured them whilst remaining fearful about the battles they would encounter ahead.

The momentum of the train made them fall asleep until Linda suddenly awoke to find herself walking through dim and dismal carriages where few passengers sat dispatched on seats with mean, evil faces.

She hurried back to her seat and tried to relax by closing her eyes, but Luck was always in her thoughts. "He seemed so happy amongst the other cats" she thought, but was still unsure if it was right for her to leave him in Cloudland.

They all slept soundly until Linda woke up again to notice a strange man wearing a large quailed hat and a large black coat that looked pale, with a mean angry face staring at her on the opposite seat.

She smiled at him, but he did not smile back she thought it strange she did not noticed him before. She closed her eyes, but all she saw in her head was this mean, angry face still starring at her. On fully opening her eyes she confirmed the man had gone. She rushed out of her seat to see where he had gone, but found herself walking to the end of the carriage that appeared to be getting further away, which left her feeling as if she was running on a treadmill because she was going nowhere.

She looked behind her to find her son and friends were out of sight; the train jerked thrashing her to the floor with the strange man standing over her.

CHAPTER 21

Emily

Meanwhile back on Earth Emily decided to call into the vet to find out how Luck was progressing. On her arrival the receptionist acted very peculiar towards her.

"Hello" She said to the smartly dressed receptionist who sat behind the desk. Emily waited for the pleasant smile she often received when she visited, but this time it was a glimpse; then the vet arrived with a peculiar look on his face.

"I'm so sorry Emily Luck is critical you must prepare for the worst." He said leaving her distraught; she only saw Luck yesterday and he was doing well. "You said he would pull through!" She questioned.

"I guess I made a mistake I need you to prepare for the worst." He continued hastily before giving her the goodbye glare.

Emily was bitterly upset to hear about Luck she desperately needed him to pull through he had become a token of hope for her because she believed that if Luck pulled through then her mother and brother would too. She hurried to the hospital dreading what she would encounter on her arrival.

On entering her mother's room she switches the radio on before sitting at her mother's bedside then suddenly there was a knock at the door that caused Emily to turn the radio down.

At the same time the doctor entered smiling warmly at her then pouring water from the jug beside her mother.

"Hello, Emily it's not god news. We have not had much improvement from your mother or your brother. I think it's time to turn the machines off" he said whilst looking to the floor. He avoided the initial shock that compelled her when raising his head; her face was pale and her eyes filled with tears she needed a few moments to gather her thoughts whilst positioning herself on the bed with her head in her hands.

"No doctor! You're making a very big mistake! I will not let you turn off those machines! I will not! She said standing firmly on her feet.

The doctor shook his head whilst watching her pitifully as she gathered every bit of strength inside her to argue, plead and reason with the doctor.

"My mother's pulse is still very strong! She will wake up! Scott just needs more time! Another week doctor that's all I'm asking and we will see what happens in a week!" She could not console herself when the thought of losing both her mother and her brother was too much for her to bear ahead of the tears streaming down her face she reached for the glass of water the doctor grasped; it trembled in her hands before she sipped it.

"We need to consider what the best course of action is we will review this in a week!" The doctor said turning towards the door.

A trembling Emily wiped her face and fixed her hair then uttered the words:

"Thank you."

Emily rushed over to her mother and shouted at her to wake up before noticing pale, lifeless Scott; she rushed over to the radio and turned the volume to maximum then she covered both ears with her hand before slumping to the floor.

The memories of them all together felt distant it had been a while since she heard her mother's voice and saw her brother's cheeky grin. She bellowed wake up as she put her head in her hands knowing it was hopeless; she turned the music down and turned the lights out before leaving.

Turning the lights off was something Emily had never done it began to worry her when she remembered how much Scott hated the dark this made her question her own actions was she finally losing hope of her mother and brother returning back to their lives? She immediately returned and switched the lights back on.

CHAPTER 22

The Earl of Dewberry

In the intervening time Linda remained unconscious her eyes flickered and the images inside her head were of thick fog which disguised a cobbled floor and old buildings that surrounded her as the heavy downpours of rain soaked her.

She lifted herself to her feet wrapping her arms around her wet, dirty clothes as she reached for her shawl abandoned on the wayside ahead of noticing the strange man emerging through the mist towards her.

"Where have you been women?" He shouted with contempt in a strong common accent,

Squeezing the residue from her shawl it was thrown over her as she rushed to greet him.

"Sorry Jim." She had a fearful glare, whilst approaching the strong smell of alcohol that shadowed him; he grabbed her by the arm and ushered her along before opening the door to a dark dismal, dwelling where a candle burned beside an injured man that was strapped to a wooden table.

The strangest thing happened when Linda saw the injured man she gave him an evil, cold glare as she watched Jim searching his pockets and taking a wallet, watches along with jewellery that he threw to her.

"Keep that safe m' darling!" Jim ordered then he pulled a gun along with a bottle of whiskey from his long black cape.

"We have got to get rid of him!" He said resting the whiskey on the table and then turning the gun towards the man.

"No Jim! They'll hang us; they'll hang us they will!" Linda shouted running between the gun and the injured man to make him put the gun away.

This was a weird experience for Linda because whilst she remained unconscious on the floor she was aware of images in her head of her reflection behaving badly, but there was nothing she could do because she had no control over it.

She continued to watch herself, becoming shocked at her actions as she questioned why would she behave that way?

"He saw us we have to get rid of him!" Jim insisted.

Linda nodded in agreement before leaving the building to hurry along the cobbled floor towards a lamppost with a horse and carriage stationed to it which she unfastened before mounting.

There were loud bangs ahead of Jim rushing out of the dwellings and joining her. "I have taken care of him." He said ahead of whipping the horse and galloping off; they were travelling through dark country lanes when they arrived at a broken down house near a farm. Jim immediately stretched his hands and demanded from Linda the items he had stolen from the man which he admired then searched the wallet to retrieve money that he stuffed into his pockets.

Once inside the farm house he barged into a room where he stood face to face with a young boy.

At the same time Linda remained unconscious and powerless, but she continued to observe all that was happening; she could not see the young boy's face because it was obstructed.

"You been doing what I said boy?" Jim shouted to a petrified boy who trembled on his presence.

"Yes sir!" the boy answered with a stutter.

"I want all the details after my supper." Jim demanded on leaving the room and seating himself at the table situated in the kitchen, where Linda prepared the supper.

The unconscious Linda continued to watch on, but was left frustrated because she was still unable to see the boy's face.

The Earl of Dewberry and his daughter Katherine was riding in the woodlands of their stately home ahead of handing the horses back to the groom.

The Earl was a very highly thought of man in the village and was very influential.

The most important person in his life was his daughter Katherine whom he often lavished with beautiful gifts.

Katherine played the piano beautiful for her father then he tucked her into bed and read her, her favourite bedtime story.

Meanwhile back on the Journey Train. It was worrying times for Jason, Charlie and Scott when they discovered Linda on the floor of the carriage with no idea how she had arrived there. A flicker of the eye lids and a twitching hand were the first signs of her coming around. She was relieved to find she had woken up from the nightmare she was having and happy to see everyone around her.

"Are you alright" Jason asked still very concerned about the state of her health.

Linda nodded; she was still quite dazed lifting herself to her feet; she thought it all very strange when she remembered her dream, but she felt it best she did not alarm anyone at this stage.

The Journey Train sped over mountains and hills before displaying views of blazing buildings and thunder storms through the blacked out windows which they all observed before drifting back asleep.

A crackling at the window awoke Linda from her sleep to discover a small girl clutching a white teddy bear outside the window; she glanced at Linda before vanishing. Linda rubbed her eyes to make sure she was not dreaming; she then discovered the girl sitting in the seat opposite her clutching her teddy whilst holding a large black key.

Linda watched in disbelief then she blinked and the little girl disappeared leaving a key on the seat.

Moments later Scott woke up to discover the key on the seat which he immediately picked up.

"No Scott!" Linda blurted, but it was too late he vanished.

Linda had witnessed everything, but became highly confused when she noticed Scott was still fast asleep on his seat; she tried to wake him up, but his lifeless body just shook whilst his watch alarmed alerting her of his low signal strength which made her extremely worried when feeling the seat where he vanished from.

There was calmness all around her then a flash of light brightened the darkened window then Jim appeared with the little girl and Scott. She raced to the window banging on it until all faces disappeared; She continued to bang the window then noticed her hand had gone straight through the glass, but it did not shatter, she tried to retrieve her hand, but instead found herself sucked through the window.

Linda found herself back in the strange place observing everything that was happening, but again unable to control anything. She was witnessing, Jim running towards the horse and carriage which was stationed to a tree with Katherine kicking and screaming in his arms when he tried to cover her mouth she bit him. He became angry then bundled her into the carriage.

Alarm bells were ringing at the home of the Earl of Dewberry when they discovered,

Katherine had been kidnapped; the Earl was devastated about his daughter's disappearance he made his views clear that he wanted his daughter back alive whatever the cost he ensured the whole village was out searching the woodlands and all the houses of convicts for her.

Katharine's mother died during childbirth leaving her father to raise her; the Earl was unable to cope with her disappearance and began drinking heavily.

There beautiful stately home grew dismal when there was no sightings of Katherine and her father riding on horsebacks through the woodlands.

The whole town was devastated to learn of the kidnap and many of the villagers and authorities agreed to join the search despite Jim demanding a large ransom and requesting the authorities were not involved.

Linda continued to observe herself sitting at the table with a large silver mug watching Jim drinking whisky.

"Scott" Jim shouted and a door flung open which left Linda gob smacked on discovering it was Scott's face that was in the room.

Scott was also the stable boy of the Earl unknown to the Earl he was also the stepson of Jim who had plotted the kidnap of Katherine. Scott was fearful that Jim would kill him should he disclose his evil plans or refuse to obey him.

A cold and frightened Katharine lay on the cold, wet floor in a cold, wet coal shed. The door unbolted when Linda entered carrying some food that she left beside her. Katherine rubbed her eyes before looking at the plate containing hard bread and scraps of meat.

"I want my daddy!" She cried.

Linda walked away bolting the door behind her leaving her crying and clutching her teddy.

Her lovely, dark, long ringlets washed away and her white dress had turned black from the coal.

When she arrived back at the house she discovered a frightened Scott sitting at the table with a drunken Jim.

"It's swarming with coppers out there, there all looking for Katherine there've stepped it up. The, Earls ordered every house be searched." Scott warned.

Jim threw his fist at the table then he turned to Linda:

"I told him no coppers! Pick up the money! It will be outside the spooked dog bar at seven o'clock. Bring it to me! I will be with the carriages on Stains

Lane! I'll come back and finish Katherine of." Jim raged then galloped down more whiskey on leaving his seat to pace up and down nervously. Linda nodded then wrapped her shawl around her as she hurriedly left with Jim.

Puddles of water were visible everywhere it was still raining heavily when there was a knock on the coal shed which alerted Katherine; causing her to sit up before wiping away tears from her eyes that were sore with crying.

"Scott is that you?" she whispered quietly.

"Katherine he'll kill you tomorrow that's what I heard him say!" Scott informed her.

Katherine screamed loudly whilst banging the wet, cold floor.

"Daddy, daddy" she screamed.

Scott tried to comfort her from the other side of the door.

"Stop crying! Once I have the key I will free you. You need to be strong Katherine." He said.

"I won't be afraid" Katherine replied whilst struggling to catch her breath.

"I will return you to your father. I promise." Scott tried to comfort her, before immediately returning to the house to look for the key. He searched all the rooms and cupboards, but he could not find it. He heard Katherine's cries which reminded him of her fate if he failed to find it. What if he could not find the key before Jim arrived? He thought as he headed back into the kitchen to notice the silver mug that Linda often drank from. He felt inside the mug to retrieve the key that was familiar to him, because it was the same key he took from the seat of the train. Scott went back to the coal shed and unlocked the door.

"Come on Katherine" Scott shouted pushing open the door which allowed Katherine to run straight into his arms.

They headed to the woodlands were they ran frantically through the woods. Then they heard Jim shouting when he discovered Katherine was gone. Scott began to panic and Katherine became very frightened.

"Hurry up Katherine! Jim's coming he will kill us both!" Scott warned, as a raging Jim galloped towards the woods.

The pair hurried through the woods, frantically as the blast of gunshots echoed from Jim riding behind them. Scott then noticed the search party ahead of them.

"Come on Katherine! You can make it!" Scott shouted, but, Katherine collapsed on the floor;

She was tired; she could not run anymore Scott tried to carry her, but she was too heavy.

It was hopeless she needed to rest. The pair stopped to rest whilst Jim's approached raging and screaming before reaching for his gun he was about to pull the trigger, when Unknown to him Linda emerged from the cart and shot him first.

The search party had almost arrived when Linda and Scott found they were awake on the Journey Train.

"Are you ok Scott?" Linda asked. Scott smiled "I had the strangest dream it was so real." He said then a raging Jim emerged in front of them causing them to back away. Scott reached for his laser which he shone and he vanished.

Eventually they settled down sucking on their coolants, as the Journey Train began to get hotter.

Linda noticed how pale Scott looked his signal strength showed three bars as opposed to six, whilst everyone had four or in Linda's case five.

Linda spooked by what she encountered with Jim and a pale and fragile Scott was causing her more concerns.

The momentum of the train rocked and shook everyone before the carriage changed to deep red as thick red clouds protruded through the dark carriage windows.

Roaring and shouting could be heard throughout the other carriages causing them to worry.

They all became alarmed when Jim emerged again wearing a long, black cape and a trilby hat.

The cape tossed two and throw as he ripped out the light fittings, then tore the seats from the carriages leaving white, fluffy stuffing flying everywhere.

Jim went silent for a while and then with a rage he appeared in front of Linda. It was Linda and Scott he wanted. He picked her up by the scruff of her neck and tossed her in the air where she spun around before landing on a pile of stuffing from the remainder of the cushions. He then flung Charlie across the floor when he tried to protect her he spun before crashing into the poles of the carriages. Jason immediately stepped in front of Scott who was trembling with fear. Jason was lifted into the air by, Jim then quick thinking Scott grabbed his laser from his pocket which he pointed towards, Jim who immediately dropped Jason to shield away from the laser, but this time the beam was to strong he was reduced to a whirl-wind that got smaller before vanishing. Miraculously everything transformed back to its original state with everyone seated back in their seat. It was almost as if nothing had happened.

"What was that all about?" Charlie asked.

"It's a long story." Linda replied.

Jason was clearly impressed with Scott when he turned towards him and said:

". . . Cheer's mate;" then patted his back.

Scott smiled he was thrilled that his quick thinking diminished Jim.

CHAPTER 23

Red Fire

The Journey Train soon came to a halt when a message came through the speakers announcing their arrival in Red Fire and instructing them to leave the train immediately.

On leaving the train there was burning smells all around them from fires blazing in holders on the platforms leaving a residue of thick red smoke visible all around the station. The thick, red dust covered the ground whilst the mist and smoke continued outside the station. After leaving the station they approached the huge, red iron gates that prized open leaving them confronted by a gigantic roller coaster climbing high into the red skies.

They followed the stony, red path to the entrance of the rollercoaster when suddenly they were distracted by the howling and barking in the distance from the beast dogs speeding towards the rollercoaster. This led to a panic from the passengers causing them to push and scramble into the cages of the roller coaster. Charlie, Jason, Linda and Scott were unable to secure a cage.

The beast dogs drew nearer as the cage slowly began to move off higher towards the skies. Below them were passengers fighting desperately for the cages as the bloodthirsty beast dogs approached snarling at the passengers that had not secured cages then pushing them onto the huge red gates.

Fearful and timid passengers formed a line against the gates whilst the sound of horse hooves galloped towards them.

Mounted on horseback was an army of rat men appearing before them their huge ears protruding through red helmets; it with their ugly, huge rat faces and long tails poking from the red suits most prominent.

They immediately dismounted to put the remaining passengers into the cages before riding away with them.

Charlie, Linda, Scott and Jason watched on through the holes of the cages engulfed by shock and horror as the heat became immense causing them to remove their jumpers and then to reach for their coolants in a bid to stop them dehydrating.

Then the rollercoaster came crashing back down directly opposite the snarling teeth and thick red tongues of the beast dogs that stalked in the red mist waiting for the roller coaster to become stationary so they could rip into the cages with their large teeth.

Launching their attack they left gaping big holes in the cages. Charlie pushed his jumper through the large hole attempting to keep the beast dogs out, but they tugged at it until they were able to force their heads through. This left them screeching and screaming whilst shielding themselves from the huge teeth of the beast dogs that had destroyed the cage. Charlie continuously tried to fend them away, but it was hopeless.

Linda screamed and Scott shouted when the beast dogs entered into the cage. Jason remembered his laser which he pointed at the beast dogs who screeched in agony before turning and running into the red mist.

The rollercoaster jerked suddenly before riding high up into the red clouds and then through high mountains, bushes and trees.

Below them were enslaved people working in the sweltering heat amongst the burning fires with sledgehammers.

Caves and blazing fires were common scenes as were whip mark were sweat and blood dripped from captives chained and beaten. It was a dismal and frightful place for the rollercoaster to halt. The beast dogs and rat men had captured many of the passengers.

On leaving the rollercoaster they found themselves amongst the thick, red dust on the grounds with blazing fires dispatched everywhere amongst the rocks and caves.

Scott, stopped to pour all the red dust from his shoes when Linda noticed how weak he was this prompted Jason to put him on his back.

They had no idea what their next encounter would be as they stopped to rest unaware of the rat men, who lingered in the red mist that miraculously all appeared.

Linda, Scott, Charlie and Jason were alarmed and frightened on their presents of the rat man, but there was nowhere to run or hide as the rat men surrounded them, forcing handcuffs and shackles on them before they too were thrown into cages .

The sweat poured off the backs of Charlie, Jason, Linda and Scott as they swung the huge sledgehammers at the rocks with shackles and handcuffs fastened to their feet and hands.

They were force to hit away at the large stones in the blazing heat, and the thick, red mist. Scott stopped to rest when the rat men lashed him with a chain that marked his back and caused him to fall to the ground.

"Get back to work!" The rat men ordered, threatening to lash him again. Scott quickly struggled to his feet. They continued working in the intense heat heavily guarded by rat men who lashed them vehemently when they stopped to rest or posed a wrong move. Linda cried when she saw the scarring on Scott's back then noticed how weak and fragile he was becoming.

"Are you ok, Scott?" She whispered wiping the tears that rolled down her cheek.

"We'll be fine mum we'll all be ok!" He said knowing his bravery would give his mother strength.

A huge, red balloon appeared before them that bust to reveal a tiny rat man jumping around in a frenzy screaming and shouting at the rat men whilst carrying a large open book.

He waved his hands vigorously and then demanded that the new arrivals taken to "Temptation City." "They are not registered." He raged.

The rat men scoured around almost immediately disarming Scott, Linda, Charlie and Jason from there shackles, thrusting them back into a dark cage and then they were taken across a red sandy desert.

They were all relieved to be leaving that evil place as they chatted inside the cage.

"That tiny man had so much power!" Scott said peeping across the cage at his mother.

Linda looked through the dark cage struggling to recognize the eyes then muttered:

"He was evil!"

The horses continued to gallop through deserts of rock and sand and burning furnaces. The immense heat left everyone exhausted, when suddenly the rat men stopped to dispatch them in what appeared a beautiful city.

CHAPTER 24

Temptation City

This city filled with large stone monuments all around whilst directly in front of them was a large building were revellers danced and loud music blasted through the walls. Jason peeped through the window of the entrance door at the people dancing, drinking and looking very merry.

"I'm just going to check this place out!" Jason said whilst pushing opens the door.

"Do you think that's wise?" Linda asked.

"I will be fine!" Jason assured her as he walked into the building leaving the others waiting outside.

On entering the building a tall man approached wearing a suit and carrying a folder he spoke with a very posh accent.

" . . . Jason I believe . . . I am Jude! Come this way!" He said leading Jason through to a bar, which had a dining area filled with people engaging in gambling activities chatting, drinking and feasting on good food.

Jason was puzzled he never knew Jude, but he appeared to know him very well.

Jude took him to a beautiful banquet room that was beautifully furnished, and then seated him around a large table lavished with fine food and drink. He soon indulged losing all recollection off his friends.

There was a beautiful young woman sat at a grand piano singing, when Jude noticed Jason's interest in the women he was hurled him towards her.

"This charming young man is Jason and this charming young lady, Eva" Jude had introduced them, before leaving them he continue to watch them until he was satisfied that, Eva had captivated him.

Meanwhile, Charlie and Linda began to get worried about Jason who had been gone for hours. After much debate it was decided Charlie would go inside to find out what had happened to him.

Jude approached Charlie immediately when he entered into the club.

". . . Hello, Charlie good of you to join us." He said putting a tick by his name from the papers that he held.

Charlie too was puzzled he could not recall ever meeting Jude as he was immediately led over to a roulette table where he was introduced to everyone at the table; it was not long before he was indulging in spirit's and given a handsome stake to participate in the roulette game and other gambling activities. Charlie became so involved that he did not remember Linda and Scott waiting outside or even his reasons for entering the building.

Linda was angry and frustrated as she banged at the club entrance.

"Charlie, Jason." She shouted, but there was no response from either of them.

Linda was becoming very concern for Charlie and Jason, but she was unsure whether to enter. She did not want to leave Scott in an unfamiliar place this was a decision she could not make easily; with great haste Linda eventually decided to enter once she assured Scott.

"I need to find out what's happened to them." She said.

"It might not be safe." Scott warned her.

"They've been gone hours." She replied.

"What if something happens to you?" Scott asked.

"I'll be fine darling! Don't worry." She said.

Scott sat on the white, stoned floor and watched his mother enter club.

A smiling chirpy, Jude brandishing champagne before introducing himself greeted Linda.

"Hello, Linda what a charming young lady you are"

He stood gaping at her for a few seconds then she was led to the banqueting area, where a feast awaited her and a charming young man sat playing her favourite song.

She watched him admiringly before her eyes met Jason across the banqueting table.

She immediately dashed towards him, but then she noticed the beautiful young woman that was charming him with her beauty. She watched on as they laughed and chatted at the end of the table until anger and jealously subdued her and she rushed over to him.

"Jason what's going on?" She shouted.

Jason looked at her strangely with dazed eyes before muttering:

"Do I know you?"

"How dare you!" She screamed whilst starring at him hard then her mind suddenly went blank causing her to lose all recollection.

"Do I know you?" Jason asked again.

"I'm sorry!" At the same time Jude ushered her back to her seat, where she continued to lavish champagne she had forgotten Scott who sat frustrated outside, waiting for his mum and friends to return.

A large shadow emerged on the floor which distracted Scott as he sat on the step at the entrance of the club he immediately thought of the beast dogs and he hid behind a stone monument arming himself with his laser. He continued to watch the shadow that seem to get larger ahead of hearing a bark that was accompanied by a small white fluffy dog limping towards him.

There was a sharp thorn stuck in the dog's leg which he quickly removed then stroked and patted him.

"Thank you" The dog said licking Scott's face.

The speaking dog alarmed Scott. He thought it crazy whilst stroking and cuddling the dog.

"Argh let go of me, your squashing me!" The dog spoke again and then he barked.

Scott immediately stopped hugging the dog and watched him harshly.

"Argh that's better" The dog said and then sighed before introducing himself to Scott.

"My name is, Doggy!" He said stretching his paw for Scott to shake.

"I'm Scott he replied shaking Doggy's paw pleasantly. .

It was not long before Doggy and Scott became fully acquainted. Doggy rolled over on his back and entertained Scott with his many tricks. He danced around, played dead and walked on two legs.

It was almost as if they had been friends for years as they played and laughed for hours. It was hard to imagine that these two had only just met, when the night sky set in and Scott was soon asleep with Doggy cuddled up beside him.

A cool breeze tickled Scott's face leaving him tossing and turning before awakening on the white stoned floor with, Doggy barking.

There was still no sign of his mum he brushed himself down before deciding to go inside the club to find out what had happened to her just as he arrived at the entrance door Doggy, stopped him.

"Wait you must not go in there!" Doggy shouted, while running ahead of him.

"Why?" Scott asked.

"You will be doomed!" Doggy warned and then jumped in front the door in a bid to stop him entering.

"My mum is in there!" He informed.

Doggy became very concerned for Scott and barked at him uncontrollably.

"She's in big trouble Scott!" He warned changing his facial expression to pity and leaving Scott very worried for his mother and his friends: "My friends are in there too!"

Doggy walked over and sat in front of him staring at a bright red sign written in blazing fire above the entrance.

"Did they not read the sign?" He asked.

Scott looked up at the sign that read: "The Club of Temptation."

"Once you have entered, you're not coming out!" Doggy continued to focus on the sign above the door.

"This place leads to so much corruption! Most people that enter are doomed for Red fire. Most of the adults in this town have entered and have been inside for years. Here in Temptation City you will find a lot of independent children" Doggy continued.

"I have to get my mum back!" Scott insisted as he walked towards the door intent on entering the club.

"Wait!" Doggy shouted as Scott again attempted to go through the entrance doors.

"There is a way of saving your mum and friends! I will help you, but you must not go through those doors!" He shouted.

"How can I save her?" Scott asked.

"There is a plant that we must find it's called the "plant of remembrance;" if we can get it we may have a chance of saving them, but it's not easy this plant is grown in the deepest of rainforest; it's a dangerous mission!" Doggy said.

"How do you know all this?" Scott asked.

"Most people think we are like Earth dogs, but we have greater intelligent than them, here in Temptation City we not only understand humans, but we can speak the language as well we haven't a moment to waste we need to find that plant!" Doggy said, but Scott was not convinced.

"You're just a dog." Scott said giving Doggy a long hard glare.

"How do I know I can trust you anyway? I have only just met you." He continued.

"You have got to trust me, Scott; you really haven't got a choice." Doggy replied.

Scott became very defensive he did not want to hear that his mum was in trouble this left him angry all he wanted was his mum back.

"I don't believe you I'm going to get my mum." He said.

Scott was determined to go through the entrance doors once more then his watched bleeped at him alerting him that he had lost another signal strength. He tried to disarm the bleeping from his watch when he mistakenly pressed the wrong button and Salmon's face appeared:

"I will try to return you to the Journey Train, but first you must be armed. If you come into any contact with the evil people, you must rebuke them. If your souls are pure, you will be destined to continue your journey. However there are many distractions and forces you will have to overcome.'

Scott listened keenly to the pre-recording which made him realize that his mum and friends may be in serious danger if he did not try to save them. He looked at Doggy who watched him pitifully how could he not trust him he thought.

"I believe you." Scott said.

Scott and Doggy ran along the stony roads of "Temptation City" until they arrived at a detached house with a strong smell of bacon coming through the opened door.

"That smells really nice and I'm really hungry." Scott said.

"Wait here" Doggy said before racing inside the house.

Scott had been waiting for a short time when Doggy came running out the house with identical boys wearing blue shorts with a yellow shirt. Both boys had thick, curly hair and were a similar age to Scott.

"This is my friend Scott who's very hungry!" Doggy said to the boys who looked at Scott then smiled.

"We are trying to get to the rain forest." Doggy continued."

"You have got to be joking." Both boys said at the same time before introducing themselves respectively.

"I am, Bill and I am, Phil, They said.

"It doesn't' matter if you can't tell us apart most people can't. If you remember one of our names then that is good enough." Both boys continued to speak at exactly the same time.

Scott was very interested and happy to meet the twins although he thought it bizarre when they both spoke together.

Scott and Doggy joined the boys for breakfast as they a sat laughing at the kitchen table whilst eating bacon and eggs and gashing down glasses of orange juice.

CHAPTER 25

Rainforest

After they had eaten their breakfast they went outside Scott jumped into the back of the land rover with Doggy whilst the twins sat on the front seats.

"What's going on?" Scott shouted nervously when he realized Phil was about to drive.

"Relax" Doggy ordered as the blue land rover raced through high woodlands, along the dusty roads onto country lanes that took them up steep hills.

They drove constantly through the night until arriving deep into the wilderness before parking beside a stream where they decided to drink some water.

Scott noticed his reflection looking at him through the stream which he thought strange. He continued to sip the water when his reflection suddenly jumped out of the water.

"What's going on?" Scott shouted as his reflection stood boldly opposite him.

"Don't be afraid of me Scott I' m your reflection." His reflection said.

Scott was stunned to be standing with his reflection before he noticed, Phil, Bill's and Doggy's reflection standing opposite them.

"You have tough times ahead of you. If you need my help at any time throughout your mission then just drink the water from this stream and I will be there to guard you. I can only rescue you once. Use me wisely!" Were the last words his reflection spoke before jumping back into the stream?

They were all left mesmerized about what their reflections told them ahead of gathering the water from the stream which they put safely in their pockets.

They decided to continue their journey by foot as they journeyed deeper into the dark rainforest.

The stars shone from the deep blue skies whilst the moonlight brightened up there route through the forest. They continued through the forest amazed by the tall trees and plants. It was then they noticed Phil climbing a stem the size of a giant beanstalk he jumped onto its huge leaf which comforted him ahead of hearing Doggy hollow to him.

"Come out! We haven't a minute to spare!" Doggy barked as Phil rolled over comfortably inside the leaf.

"I'm tired!" Phil shouted as he continued to slumber inside the leaf making it apparent to them that it was time for a rest; it wasn't long before they were all slumbered in the comfort of large leaves.

With eyes fixed on squirrels running up the trees whilst tiny birds dug for worms they had awaken from a good night sleep. When they each rolled over they were met by long, black beaks belonging to enormous, white eagles with fur like snow surrounding them.

Afraid that they were to be captured were their thought ahead of the leaf slowly closing to protect them from the dangers that were detected, but Bill's leaf struggled to close leaving him in full view of an eagle that flew towards him before capturing him in its large beak.

A terrified Bill was tightly gripped in the eagle's beak.

When all the eagles were out of sight the petals reopened for them to discover Bill, was missing; they looked to the skies to glimpse the eagle disappearing with him.

Everyone was speechless before a loud wailing from Phil. He was uncontrollable he had never been without Bill.

"What if I never see him again?" Phil sobbed.

They all pondered, but did not have a clue what to say or even how they would get, Bill back.

"Don't worry! We will find your brother." Scott said.

Phil continued to weep his face filled with sadness when Doggy barked frantically.

"There is hope! He still has his water "Doggy said.

They immediately smiled whilst listening intensively while Doggy continued to speak.

"There is hope that Bill could return safely if he drinks the water from the stream.

"If he's got any sense he will drink the water." Phil said he seemed a bit more cheerful as he rubbed his eyes:

"Bill is very intelligent. I'm sure he'll find a way to escape the eagles clutches." Phil continued.

The eagle glided to her nest occupied with ostrich sized babies simultaneously thrusting Bill towards them viciously prodded him before the eagle glided away.

Bill covered in multitude of cuts and bruises because of fending them off had suddenly remembered the water that slipped and lodged on the edge of the nest when he tried to reach for it; the eagles continued to peck at him he turned and used his strength to fend them off before retrieving and sipping the water.

Moments after his reflection appeared like a genie from a bottle.

"Your wish is my command." The reflection uttered while floating around the nest on a huge cloud.

The baby eagles screeched and scrambled out of the nest falling to the ground one by one on sight of the huge reflection. There angry mother heard there cries and flew at full speed to protect them.

"Take me back to my brother!" Phil shouted as the eagle appeared to discover she had lost her baby eagles.

On her arrival Bill vanished leaving the angry eagle flapping and squawking crazily.

Phil was delighted when his brother appeared standing beside him covered in cuts and bruises.

"I can now tell you apart now." Scott joked on noticing Bill's injuries as they continued their journey deeper into the rain forest searching every plant hoping it would be the plant of remembrance, but each time doggy, shook his head.

"How will we know when we find it?" Scott asked.

"According to the myth we will know and it will find us" Doggy replied.

They continued searching the rainforest studying every plant, before tasting them; then Doggy began to bark loudly at a tunnel he had just discovered hidden beneath unkempt shrubbery.

"I thought you had found it." Scott shouted after racing over to Doggy.

"Be Quiet!" Doggy ordered as he stared mysteriously at the tunnel. Then suddenly a bright light began to beam which left them all bewildered.

"What is it?" Scott, whispered.

Be quiet!" Doggy said again.

The bright light began to shine brighter ahead of it suddenly transforming into a ball which ejected directly in front of them. They were mystified by it whizzing around in the air like a bumble bee, before bouncing up and down as it settled on the ground to transform into one of the most beautiful women ever seen; she had skin like honey and silky, black hair her eyes shone like a star. She stood wearing a green satin swimsuit that camouflaged her with the plants.

"I am, Leila the plant of remembrance." She announced.

They all stood enlightened by her amazing beauty.

Scott stepped forward.

"I'm Scott! This is Doggy and here you have the twins Phil and Bill." As he pointed at them respectively they all stepped forward and greeted, Leila with a smile and a warm hello.

Leila seemed warm and friendly when she approached them in turn touching and kissing each of their cheeks.

"What brings you here?" She asked.

Scott stepped forward once more still blushing from the peck on his cheek.

"My mum and my friends have entered the "the Club of Temptation." The only hope I have of saving them will be to find the plant of remembrance."

"Who told you of such a plant?" Leila asked leaving all eyes focused on, Doggy urging him to explain himself.

"I did." Doggy said.

"So you have been searching for this plant?" Leila asked.

They all nodded ahead of Leila laughing out loudly at them which left them feeling intimidated.

"Did you taste any plants in the forest?" She asked.

They all nodded and again she laughed aloud.

"Do you not remember my name?" She asked they looked at each other then became embarrassed as none of them had remembered her name.

"I'm, Leila the plant of remembrance it is I you search!" She said again with a chuckle.

"But . . . You're not a plant!" Scott said.

"We are all plants of the Earth." She said.

"Can you help me?" Scott pleaded.

"I want to help you, but I must not leave this place unless I return in a few hours or I will lose all my powers." Leila said.

Scott knew all hope was lost and turned to Doggy.

"It's taken us days to arrive here all hope is lost Leila will never return in a few hours if we took her to Temptation City what can we do now, Doggy?' Scott asked.

Doggy shook his head he had no idea.

"I'm sorry! I really thought we were searching for a plant that we could take back with us." Doggy said when an enthusiastic Bill suddenly began to shout.

"The water" Bill shouted as they all listen keenly.

"Here's the plan we have three bottles of water left. We can wish for us to be safely transported back to Temptation City and then for Leila's safe return." Bill continued.

"We will save the last bottle in case of any emergencies, but first we need to get back to the Land rover; at least that way we are all in one place. They all boarded the land rover when large eagles began landing feet away from them that forced them out. It was the angry eagle that had returned she stalked out Bill then; she flew towards him violently before trying to capture him; he continued to dodge away by rolling around the floor and hiding behind the tall trees.

She continued flying towards him intent on harming him whilst he continued to dodge her and then more eagles appeared intent on attacking them; they all began to dodge them as they gave chase around the forest.

Scott was aghast when he saw Doggy captured in the beak of one of the eagles who was about to fly off with him. He reached for his bottle of water, but instead found his laser which he shone at the eagle that immediately dropped Doggy before flying off.

Scott continued to point his laser at all the eagles until they had flown away.

They returned to the land rover and Phil drank the water that beckoned his reflection appearance.

"Hello, Phil I'm here to help you in times of need I can only help you once!" his reflection said.

Phil was astonished at how similar they were. It was hard for him to accept that this was actually him. The reflection waited patiently for him to stop coughing. They all watched on cautiously looking for signs of birds or any other dangerous animals when Phil took another sip of the water to ease his cough.

"Please take us all back to "Temptation City" Phil said.

The land rover immediately appeared back in Temptation City. The sound of joy and happiness on their return was cut short when Doggy reminded them that their mission was not yet over.

"Leila must be returned on time and Scott's mother and friends are still in danger. We have no time to waste!" Doggy warned before turning to Phil sitting in the driver's seat.

"Phil you must take us to the "Club of Temptation Bar immediately!" Doggy ordered.

Phil speeded towards the Club of Temptation. When they arrived they were all about to enter the club.

"No one must go in there except Leila." Doggy said they all stepped back and allowed Leila to enter the Club of Temptation.

"I will do my best!" Leila said.

A strong wind accompanied Leila on her entrance to the club that blew people over and turned over tables. People struggled to find their feet as the wind got stronger.

Jude hurried to greet Leila, but like a treadmill he remained at the same spot.

The pianist suddenly stopped playing the piano when everyone exited the banquet blown towards the exit of the club.

The wind began to blow mildly which caused everyone to find their feet and continue in their usual role for a short while then the wind got stronger which caused the chefs to stop cooking, the waiter left the trays which they carried.

Everyone stopped what they were doing as they all began to remember. Many people had been inside the club for years and had no recollection of their former lives.

Jason tore away from the singer he was tempted by and quickly left the club.

Charlie grabbed all his chips from the roulette table and rushed to collect his winnings, but was angry when he discovered all the cashiers had gone.

He quickly rushed towards the exit when he witnessed a sharp punch hit the face of a drunken man who touched Linda's buttocks.

"How dare you!" She shouted as the man squirmed at her.

"That hurt." He said holding his face.

Charlie grabbed her at the same time ushered her out of the club.

"Come on, Linda let's get out!" He shouted.

They were ashamed of their actions once they were all outside the club and then Linda became frantic on realizing Scott was missing.

"Where is Scott?" She screamed.

Everyone looked around frantically then Linda decided to enter the club again.

No you must not go back in there!" Charlie warned grabbing her arm in a bid to stop her.

It was difficult for Scott to find his mother and friends because of all the people leaving the club.

Scott was also very concerned about his mother and friends and was unsure if they managed to escape he decided to stand on the roof of the land rover which enabled him to see his mother and friends. He jumped off and then pushed his way through the crowds until he found them.

Leila was happy to see Scott reunited with his mum and friends when she came out of the club.

"Thank you, Leila." Scott said; soon after Leila was transformed back into a ball that shone brightly. Scott picked up the ball and carried it back to the land rover. He was about to beckon his reflection when Doggy stopped him.

"Wait I need to come with you so you can come back!" Doggy told him. Scott was puzzled, but soon realized what Doggy was saying:

"We needed that last bottle of water after all" He was surprised he did not realize that he would need to come back to Temptation City after returning Leila to the rainforest.

Doggy accompanied Scott in the land rover. Scott drank the water and his reflection appeared. Linda, Charlie and Jason stared in amazement whilst Scott spoke to his reflection.

"Could you transfer everyone in the land-rover safely back to the rain forest, please" Scott asked.

There was a tiny whirlwind were the land rover once stood. Then moments later it returned with Scott and Doggy.

CHAPTER 26

Leaving Temptation City

The watches alerted them that the Journey Train was in the vicinity on checking their signal strength; it was very low for both Charlie and Scott. They knew time was running out they needed to get out of Red Fire and this city and make their way home.

Scott was very sad to be leaving his friends he was going to miss Doggy dreadfully.

"Thank you for helping me." Scott said as Doggy licked him all over his face.

"I'm really going to miss you . . ." Oh I wish I could take you with me." Scott continued.

"I'll miss you to Scott!" Doggy said.

They all got in the blue land rover and Bill handed the keys to Jason. He had given them the land rover so they could return to the Journey Train.

"I'm going to miss you all." Scott said as he patted and kissed Doggy for the last time; he reached for a final hug from the twins then Jason started the engine.

Charlie, Linda and Scott all waved as they left "Temptation City"

They were driving for a long time. Temptation city seemed a distant place as they journeyed through hills, valleys and along stony, sandy roads before noticing the rollercoaster far in the distant that would take them back to the station.

There was only one stop visible on the board when they entered inside the station "Earth" was the only visible destination.

They were all very happy when the train arrived to take them home.

"We are almost home now." Linda said as they paced around the waiting room eagerly then Scott suddenly collapsed on the floor he looked very weak as his watch let off a high pitch bleep. Linda discovered there was only one bar remaining that was intermittently fading causing his watch to bleep loudly.

Linda panicked whilst comforting him on the floor as Jason rushed over and carried him onto the platform.

"What if he does not make it?" Linda asked.

"He'll be fine! I can hear the train coming now!" Jason continued as the train pulled into the platform; when the doors opened they were confronted by more rat men who immediately ambushed Jason with him still holding Scott.

Charlie grabbed Scott then forced himself on to the train in the scuffle then shouted to Linda: "Get on the train!"

Linda jumped on the train watching helpless as the evil rat men were about to take away Jason.

She refused to leave him in the clutches of the evil rat men.

"Leave him alone!" She shouted at them, but they continued to drag him away.

"Get off me!" Jason shouted as he struggled hysterically in a bid to free himself.

The doors tried to close, but Linda stopped them by refusing to move out of the way this made, Charlie shout anxiously at her.

"There is nothing we can do!" Charlie yelled.

Linda searched her bag recklessly for her laser, but was unable to find it.

"Stop, leave him alone!" She shouted, but the rat men left the platform leaving her distraught. Charlie continued to shout too Linda:

"Come on Linda . . . The train is ready to leave." He shouted to her, but she was still at the doors of the carriage refusing to move.

"Let the door's close!" Charlie demanded, but she still refused to move away from the door.

"Scott's in danger! Your children need you!" Charlie shouted.

Linda slowly walked into the carriage to join Charlie and Scott nonetheless the thought of Jason left in Red fire at the mercy of the evil rat men was too much for her to bear.

"Jason risked everything to save us we cannot leave him like that." She said to Charlie who hugged her; he to felt sad about what happened to

Jason, but he only had one bar left on his signal strength and he would not risk returning to Earth to save him.

The doors were about to close again when Linda rushed off towards them.

"I have to go back for Jason! We cannot leave him here! You and Scott go back to Earth. I've got enough signal strength I will try and rescue him." She said whilst rushing out the train doors.

Charlie was very concerned because she was risking not returning to Earth.

"Linda, you can't take on the rat men all by yourself!" He warned.

"I have to do something! Give me the lasers and the coolants." She insisted leaving Charlie, searching frantically through Scott's pockets and then his own for the lasers that he retrieved, along with the coolants which he threw to her just before the train doors closed.

The train jerked and a voice came over the speaker notifying them of the train's departure. Linda stood alone on the platform waving to Charlie and Scott whilst the train pulled away.

Charlie and Scott were asleep for most of the journey, when they were awakened by a loud audible noise.

"All those wishing to depart at this station must sit patiently on the benches in the waiting area. There are no exit gates at this station you must be seated in the seating area and the transitions will occur in due course."

The train doors opened and the passengers began to exit the train. Charlie was weak, but continued to carry a fragile Scott through to the waiting area towards the rows of benches positioned on the walls.

The waiting area was a long corridor with bland walls, high ceilings; there was a sense of calmness all around them as they seated themselves on the benches amongst the other passengers.

"Where's my mum?" Scott asked.

Charlie wiped away a tear after Scott spoke he was very sad that Linda was not with them.

"She'll be on the next train Scott! Don't you worry?" He said as they both rested on the benches until they fell into a deep sleep.

Meanwhile back at the hospital Emily sat in the doctor's office waiting for the doctor to arrive.

"Hello, Emily" the doctor said as he entered into his office.

Emily smiled nervously at him knowing she needed to be strong, but could not control her tears.

"Your mother's pulse is still very strong Emily, but little Scott his losing his battle his pulse is very weak. We need to consider what the best course of action is now we may not have any alternative, but to switch of the life support!" The doctor concluded.

Emily became very distraught because she could not imagine life without her little brother.

"No doctor, she said! You cannot do that! We have to give him more time!" She demanded.

"I'm afraid that's impossible we have other patients requiring the machine. I am sorry, Emily. I've instructed the team to switch off the equipment in a few hours." He proclaimed.

Emily was heartbroken and devastated as she cried uncontrollably on her chair.

"Please, let me say goodbye. Let me see if I can bring him back one last time." She begged.

"I will grant you an hour, Emily, but we cannot delay it any further!" The doctor reasoned.

Emily rushed to Scott's bedside where she sat beside him stroking his pale face.

"I will always love you my darling brother. Life will never be the same again." She whispered and then softly kissed his cheek before singing his favourite lullaby:

"Dah de dah de da, mmmmmmmmmmh." She sang. She stopped singing and starred at his lifeless face.

"You will always be my brother and I will always love you wherever you are." She whispered.

The tears came streaming down her cheeks when she realized his dreams would soon be gone.

Emily turned away she shuddered with fear as she could not bear to see Scott that way she walked towards the door then stopped on hearing a cough, which caused her to look back to see Scott coughing.

"Oh, Scott you came back! Darling, you came back." She cried as she hurried over to kiss and hug him she pressed the emergency knob then shouted: "Nurse, nurse." When no one arrived she rushed through the corridors "Nurse, nurse" she yelped desperate to speak with any hospital staff on reaching the reception she was like a child opening the perfect gift at Christmas.

"Nurse, nurse; He's back." She shouted to all the nurses sitting behind the desk as they all looked at her thinking she had lost her mind.

"Come I'll show you" Emily said gesturing with her hand excitedly at the same time the nurses insisting that she calm down.

The nurse followed her to Scott there was no movement except his eyes were twitching leaving the nurse stunned by his return.

"I'm very pleased for you, Emily." The nurse said as they rushed over to him and began dismantling the wires attached.

"It's the second good news today we had a man in the room a few doors away came back a few minutes ago his wife is over the moon." She continued while making Scott comfortable in his bed. There was a big smile from Emily when Scott opened his eyes.

"I had the most amazing dream." He muttered.

"What did you dream about" Emily asked.

"Urn . . . I can't remember." He replied.

Emily was overwhelmed that Scott had come back, but she was still very sad because her mother lay just in the bed next to him and she was still in a coma.

CHAPTER 27

Return

Linda continued her quest to save Jason by boarding the land rover armed with her laser; she was unaware of the pack of beast dogs gathering speed in the distance that was racing towards her. On reaching her she found herself apprehended by them. Her lateral thinking made her retrieve her laser that she immediately shone at them leaving them whimpering before fleeing. She was now free to board the rollercoaster that took her back through the mountains and valleys until she arrived at the caves where they had all been enslaved.

On entering the cave she could smell the furnace whilst the clamours of hammers got louder. She took refuge behind a stone to avoid the rat men and the beast dogs. She knew she must not fall asleep as there were rat men and beast dogs everywhere. Then alarmed by a rustling noise in the bushes outside the cave she continued to hide behind the stone whilst armed with her laser as the noise got louder.

Linda braced herself ready with her laser when to her surprise she saw a black cat coming towards her as the cat approached her she immediately recognized him.

"Hello, Luck." She said whilst stretching her hand for Luck to lick then she noticed how thin and dehydrated he looked she reached for her coolants which Luck licked and chewed then Linda searched her bag for a bottle of water which she scooped in her hand for him to sip.

"Oh you poor thing" She whispered.

Linda was surprised to have found Luck who was clearly on a mission to get back to Earth. She popped Luck into her bag after deciding it was time to rescue Jason.

She entered deep inside the cave which became hotter from a river of larvae that flowed through the rocks.

Most of the captives were slumped in awkward positions asleep on rocks whilst the rat men were parading the caves.

It was very unpleasant to see the captives laying there with lash marks on their backs and sweet pouring off them. Linda afraid she might be captured; continued to crouch down behind a rock when she heard a voice calling out to her.

"Help me." The voice said.

She looked around to discover a captive squashed beneath two rocks still chained with sweat whip marks and scars covering his face and back. Linda managed to free him from the rocks.

"Thank you" He said and stretched his hand for her to shake.

"Lukas." He said.

Linda shook his hand still chained to shackles before looking for her laser in her bag that she used to break the shackles.

He immediately pushed her on to a rock and snatched the laser leaving her unconscious on the floor.

Lukas raced through the caves freeing all the captives with the laser until he approached Jason still chained to his shackles; his face was black from the soot in the caves and he had fresh wounds on his back Jason was happy to be freed which enabled him to immediately retrieve his laser; he became suspicious when he noticed the laser.

"Where did you get that laser?" Jason questioned.

"I found it." Lukas said continuing to free many more captives.

A fierce battle between the captives and rat men commenced as Jason and Lukas dashed towards the exit of the cave to be confronted by the rat men. that they beamed with the lasers. Jason was about to leave the cave with Lukas when he was alerted by Luck,

"Meow meow" Luck meowed loudly.

". . . Luck." He said.

He tried to grab him, but he ran back into the cave and Jason followed while Lukas left the cave.

Jason could see mass destruction everywhere. There were injured captives and dead rat men everywhere. Jason continued to follow Luck across an iron bridge he tried to reach for his laser, but it fell over the bridge; he was apprehended by the rat men that tried to heave him into the river of larvae. Jason was left hanging by his fingers over the bridge with the rat men about to kick his hand that clung desperately on to the edge of the bridge.

Linda emerged shinning the laser directly at the rat man as she tried to rescue Jason hanging from the bridge.

She was unaware it was Jason as she hauled him back onto the bridge he was giving coolants and water, before wiping away the thick soot that smothered his face.

"Jason." She said ecstatic that she had found him as she watched him recover soon after chewing on the coolant.

Once over the bridge they were in full view of the rat men charging towards them. They both shone the laser that dispersed them as they raced to the exit to be met by Luck.

"Meow" Luck meowed again and Jason picked him up and they all ran as fast as they could away from the caves towards the roller coaster they rested for a short time drinking water and chewing the coolant while they waited for the roller coaster to arrive.

They knew they must not fall asleep because the rat men were everywhere and the beast dogs were in hunt for their blood.

They heard horses galloping when they looked behind them to see the rat men charging down on Lukas who tried to activate the laser which had broken; the rat men captured him and bungled him into the carts whilst Linda and Jason remained huddled behind the rock.

The rollercoaster sped off with Linda and Jason; on arriving at the station the Journey Train was waiting filled with captives that had escaped the clutches of the rat men.

Once they boarded the train the doors closed and the train sped off with them.

The End